MW00929633

CHASING
SERENITY

An Inspirational Romance Novel

Taretha Jones

Chasing Serenity

DEDICATION

I'd like to thank first and foremost, God. Without HIM I would not have had the courage and drive to complete this work.
I'd like to thank my parents, who taught me the value of reading and writing, at an early age.
I would also like to thank the remainder of my family for their love and support.

Chasing Serenity

THE STORYLINE

Twenty-six year old Serenity Walker is the beautiful single mom to a precocious five-year old son. Forced to deal with a deceitful boyfriend who wants nothing to do with the child they created together, she decides to raise her son alone...it's just her and God.

In her attempts to carve a life for herself as a professional chef, she has no real desire for a man in her world. That all changes when she meets ex-football player Jason Bullock.

Burned by a past relationship, Jason is not really looking to give his heart away again. As God would have it, that all changes when he meets Serenity. It's practically love at first sight for Jason and all out resistance for her. Jason knows their love is special, so he's willing to fight for Serenity. Even if it means putting up a chase.

Chasing Serenity

$\mathcal{C}$HAPTER 1

"Oooooh, girl...he's coming over here."

Twenty-two year old Serenity Walker looked up from her plate of beef-fried rice at her friend, Jasmine. Then she looked around in confusion — she didn't see anybody that *she* knew. "*Who's* coming over here, Jasmine?"

"The hottie — the one who said hi to us when we first came into the mall."

Serenity shook her head and went back to eating her meal. She'd known Jasmine ever since their freshman year in college. That had been four years ago. In other words, she was used to Jasmine talking about some hottie or another.

Seconds later, when they heard an unfamiliar masculine voice say, "Hello, ladies," Serenity didn't even bother to look up from her plate.

Jasmine on the other hand, gave the stranger a dazzling smile. "Hello yourself."

The man was quick to introduce himself. "I'm Jonathan. I'm a lab tech at A&T in the chemistry department. I think I've seen you two lovely ladies around campus."

The man looked directly at Serenity. "I remember seeing *you* last semester. You took an eight-o'clock morning class...Professor Ramsuddin's session I believe."

At that point, Serenity finally looked up at the stranger. She had to admit that Jasmine was right — he was exceptionally good-looking.

The muscular brown-skinned man continued speaking to Serenity. "Yep, I certainly do remember you...I'd never forget a beautiful face like yours."

Even though his comment vaguely had the feel of a stale pickup line, for some reason, Serenity decided to humor him anyways and reply. She gave him a tiny smile. "Is that so?"

He nodded his head. "Definitely."

"Well, thank you I guess."

Jasmine giggled. "I'm gonna save us all some time and just cut to the chase. My friend here is single...that is if you're interested in taking her out on a date."

Serenity could have kicked Jasmine under the table at that point.

Jonathan couldn't help but smile. "I would love to go out on a date with your friend, but first I think I need to at least know her name."

"Her name's Serenity."

Looking at Serenity the entire time, he nodded his head. "Serenity...that's a beautiful name. I like it."

Jasmine decided to continue with her attempts to get her girl a hook-up. "My boyfriend and I are gonna catch that new Fast Lane movie this Friday. You seem decent enough. Maybe the four of us could make it a double date."

Serenity wasn't really feeling the way the two of them were talking about her — making plans as if she weren't sitting right there in their presence.

"What do you say, Serenity? You think you'll give a lonely, single guy like myself a chance?"

Jasmine grinned. "Yeah, Serenity. You giving him a chance?"

Serenity sighed. A tiny little voice in her head was telling her to just say no. In fact the word was on the tip of her tongue. Therefore she was surprised herself when she heard herself say, "Yes."

* * *

Two Months Later:

Betty Walker frowned as her daughter came into the living room where she was sitting watching the evening news. "You going out with that boy again?"

Serenity sighed. "Yes I am, mama. I just don't understand why you don't like Jonathan."

Betty shook her head. "It's something about him, Serenity. I don't know exactly what it is myself. But the Lord done put on my spirit that that boy means no good for you, baby. He's only gonna bring you hurt and harm."

Mama's just tripping, she thought to herself as she bent down to give her mother a quick peck on the cheek. Sure enough, Serenity herself had been hesitant to go out with Jonathan in the beginning...when they'd first met that day at the mall. But now she was happy that Jasmine had forced her hand.

It was at that moment that they both heard a car's horn honking outside of the house. Serenity grabbed her purse from off of the sofa. "Don't wait up for me tonight, Mama. I'm coming home late."

Betty simply shook her head as her only child ran out of her house. "Lord...that boy was sent from Satan. I know it! Please protect my child."

Chasing Serenity

* * *

Jonathan started complaining as soon as Serenity got into his car. "What took you so long coming out of your mama's house?"

Serenity frowned. "I came out as soon as I heard you blow, Jonathan."

He pulled out into the city street. "Your mama don't like me do she, girl?"

Serenity was raised up in the church, so she refused to just outright lie. She shook her head and smiled at her man. "She just doesn't know you like I do, bae. That's all. Once she gets to know you better, the two of you will be like old friends."

Jonathan shook his head. He highly doubted that. He felt like telling Serenity how he really felt about her scowling-face mama, but he knew she'd never let him get into the panties if he did that. And getting between Serenity's legs is exactly what he wanted. It's the reason he'd been paying for dates and movies for the last two months while getting nothing but some kisses in return. But he had plans to change all of that.

He took a quick glance over at the girl sitting in his passenger-side seat. Then he felt a familiar stirring in his nether regions. *From the top of her head, to the tip of her toe she's fine.*

He quickly decided to change the subject from her mama. He was pretty sure if he kept talking about that old bat, his plans for the entire evening would be ruined.

Minutes later, he pulled into the parking lot of a Motel 6.

Serenity frowned. "Why are we here, Jonathan? I thought we were going to the movies."

He reached across his console and took her hand into his. "It's my birthday tomorrow, bae. Since I'm gonna be out of town, I figured you could give me my gift early."

"I already bought you a gift. It's at my momma's house."

He gave her hand a gentle squeeze. "You know I'm in love with you, don't you Serenity? I was hoping you'd be with me this evening as my gift." He brushed the back of his hand softly across the side of her face. "I don't want to wait until the day we get married. I love you and I want to show you how much. I want you to *feel* how much I love you."

She had her reservations about what he was asking of her, but she'd never had anyone besides her mama tell her that they loved her.

"Please, Serenity, baby...I love you."

"You do?"

10

"Yes, sweetheart. Just let me show you how much. Okay?"

She sighed. Then she nodded her head. "Okay."

* * *

Later on that Evening:

As much as he wanted to stay in that cheap motel room and hit it again, Jonathan knew he had to leave and take his piece of new booty home. He began putting back on his clothes. Then he turned to Serenity. "You were good, baby. But now I'm gonna need you to get dressed. I have a long day tomorrow, seeing that I'm going out of town to visit my sick grandmother. We have to get going. I have to take you home."

Serenity frowned. She was feeling guilty. Everything her mama had ever told her about not sleeping with a man who wasn't her husband came to her mind.

Seeing her crestfallen face, he decided to change his approach to her a little. He smiled to himself while thinking, *I've got to soften her up and lay a path for the next time I want to hit it — which I know will be very soon.*

He came over and gave her a hug. "I know you're the one for me, Serenity. Don't worry, we're gonna have

11

a lifetime of staying in bed together once we get married."

"Married?" she asked, then smiled.

"Yeah, girl. You're the one. I know it. Like I told you before...I see us getting married. Now go ahead and hurry up and get your clothes on."

Starting to feel good from what Jonathan had just revealed to her, Serenity was happy to oblige.

*C*HAPTER 2

Over the next several weeks, Serenity spent a good deal of time going out with Jonathan. She was even convinced that she'd fallen in love. She smiled to herself. The fact that he would tell her on an almost daily basis that he loved her, too...that they would be together forever...had made falling for him easy.

"Hey, Serenity. I'd like you to meet Catina Grey. She's my friend from work — the one I was telling you about."

Serenity had just climbed into the passenger-side seat of Jasmine's car. She looked towards the back seat at the girl sitting there and smiled. "Hi, Catina. It's good to finally meet you. Jasmine has been saying a lot of good things about you."

As she backed her car out of Serenity mom's driveway, Jasmine grinned. "Like I was telling you before we got here, Catina, I'm surprised my girl Serenity here agreed to help us cater my cousin's party tonight."

Serenity looked across at Jasmine with a confused expression on her face. "Why are you surprised about that, Jasmine?"

"Because, boo...you've been spending all your free time with Jonathan. I hardly every get to see my bestie anymore."

Serenity couldn't disagree. She couldn't say anything to the contrary because what Jasmine had just said had been the truth.

Jasmine smiled. She reached over and patted Serenity on the hand. "It's okay, honey. I ain't mad at you. I know what it feels like to be in love for the first time. I felt the exact same way about Kevin — that is until we broke up."

Serenity shook her head. "Jonathan and I are never breaking up. We're getting married."

"Married?!"

Serenity nodded her head. "Yeah. We haven't set a date yet...or gotten officially engaged. But that's what he keeps talking about all the time." She smiled. "Yep, he said that I'm the one and that we're getting married one day."

Sitting in the back seat, Catina grimaced. "I dated a guy named, Jonathan, once. He used to shoot me the same lines...that is until I found out about his wife."

Serenity looked back at Catina. "Oh, dang, girl. That's messed up. I'm sorry that you had to go through that."

Catina, with her lips set in a thin, angry line said, "Yeah, thanks Serenity. I'm sorry I had to go through it, too."

Jasmine shook her head. "I tell you, ladies...I don't care what anybody says differently...good guys are hard to find."

Catina couldn't agree more. "Oh, I know that's right. The good ones aren't *hard* to find...it's more like they're impossible to find." She let out a breath on an angry sigh. "But finding buttwipes like Jonathan Broadnax is easy."

Serenity pulled her eyebrows together in a frown. "Did you say Jonathan *Broadnax*?"

Catina nodded her head. "Yeah. Jonathan Antoine Broadnax the second. He works as a chemistry lab assistant at A&T." She paused. "What? You know him or something?"

Serenity felt her heart tighten in her chest. *It can't be*, she thought to herself. *There's no way we could be talking about the same person. It's impossible.*

Jasmine was just as shocked as Serenity. But she knew it had to be him. Why? Because the chances of two

15

Jonathan Antoine Broadnaxes the second working at the university in a chemistry lab were slim to none. Trying to keep her cool and assume the positive, she said, "Maybe he's not married anymore, Serenity."

Catina shook her head. "If we're talking about the same person, then I highly doubt that. I broke up with his behind about eight months ago — when his wife somehow found out about me and showed up at my house. I'm pretty much sure they're still married. I didn't know it, of course, but I was just the sidechick. According to wifey, he done pulled the same crap several times."

Serenity was numb. She didn't even notice Jasmine turning the car around and heading back towards her mother's house. Not until she'd parked along the curb.

Jasmine cut her Camry's engine. "Catina and I can come inside with you to your room if you want us to, honey."

Serenity slowly shook her head. "No. You need to go help your cousin throw that party. She's depending on you to show up." Unshed tears burned the back of her eyelids. "Plus...I...I need to be alone."

With that being said, Serenity pulled open the car door and ran into the house.

Jasmine narrowed her eyes. Then she thinned her lips

in anger. "I suddenly feel like slashing some tires or putting some sugar in somebody's tank. You know where Jonathan lives Catina?"

"Yeah. Over off of Patterson Street." Catina shook her head. "But trust me, girl...fooling around with trying to pay him back ain't a good idea. His wife is crazy."

"Crazy?"

"Yeah. When she found out about me, I had to take a restraining order out on her behind." She paused then continued speaking. "I recommend staying far away from both of them...as far away as possible."

* * *

Serenity stayed locked up in her bedroom for two whole days. Jonathan had called her the night she'd found out about his deception. He hadn't even tried to deny the truth — that he was a married man. That he'd lied to her about being single and unattached.

She frowned when she heard her mother knocking softly on her bedroom door. "Serenity, now I don't know what's going on with you. And I know you're twenty-two — that you're a grown woman. But you've been holed up in there two days now. Baby, open the door. Let mama in...we need to talk."

Serenity stood up from her bed. She walked over and opened the door. With her eyes puffy from crying, she stared at her mother for only a few seconds then said, "You were right mama...Jonathan's no good. He's married and I'm pregnant."

Betty wanted to pull her only child into her arms — it was on her heart to do so — but she just couldn't bring herself to do it. She shook her head instead. "Lord, Serenity. I brought you up in the church — gave you every advantage that I possibly could. I tried to warn you 'bout that boy — that he was sent straight from the devil — and now you got his baby growing in your belly?"

It was hard for her to do so, but Betty turned on her heel and walked away from her daughter. Not even Serenity's loud sobs made her turn back around. With her heart heavy, she went to her bedroom. *I wanted a better life for her than I had for myself, and now she done went and ruined it all.*

Betty pulled out her Bible, but didn't open it. She placed the holy book back on her nightstand and began to sob herself.

It took several minutes for Serenity to find the strength to step back into her bedroom. She closed the bedroom door behind herself then sank down to the carpet. Jonathan had betrayed her in the worst possible way and now her mother had turned her back on her. She was hurting so bad that she felt like she wanted to die.

* * *

Three Days Later:

Betty frowned. Then she cut her eyes at her best friend of twenty-five years — Carla — who was also the assistant pastor at their church. "What do you mean by I'm wrong, Carla?"

Carla shook her head. "What I mean, Betty, is that she's your child. And yes her fornicating and getting herself knocked up is wrong. But Serenity's a good kid...a good daughter." She pursed her lips together then continued speaking. "We've all sinned and fallen short of the Father's glory." She pointed at Betty. "Plus, I remember twenty-three years ago you found yourself in a similar situation."

Betty shook her head. "But I wasn't raised up in the church like Serenity was. I had Serenity's butt in a pew every Sunday...my mama let me run wild in the streets. Serenity should have known better."

Carla frowned. "Betty, you know the devil's always working, and he's got his old evil eye on the righteous in particular. We serve a merciful God. If Serenity is willing to repent of her sins — which I'm sure she is 'cause she's got a good heart — the Lord will forgive her. Now why can't you? Why can't you forgive your child?"

* * *

It had been a whole week since the night her mother had come to her room and the strained relationship they now shared was almost unbearable. So much so that Serenity had made the difficult decision to move out.

Betty frowned as she watched her only daughter taking bag after bag out to her car. When Serenity slung her purse over her shoulder and was about to walk out the front door for the last time, Betty's mind flashed back to the conversation she'd had with Carla the day before. Then she said, "Serenity...wait."

Serenity frowned. Facing the front door, she refused to turn around. She didn't want to see the look of hate and disappointment that she was sure was in her mother's eyes. She'd seen it for what felt like a million times too many already. "What is it, mama?"

"Have you cut off your relationship with that boy?"

"He's married...I know that now. Of course I have, mama."

Betty nodded her head. "Good." Then she paused.

Then she let a tired breath out on a sigh. "Serenity, I don't want you to move out. Now don't get me wrong — I don't like this situation — but the Lord can still forgive you and bless you and my grandchild."

Serenity couldn't believe what she thought her mother had just said. *Did I hear her right*, she thought to herself. Then out loud she said, "Can you repeat that please, mama?"

"I said I don't want you to move out, child. I want to help you get through this."

Serenity hadn't really wanted to leave the home that she'd spent most of her childhood in. In fact, she'd planned on roughing it out in her car for a while — seeing that she didn't have anywhere else to go. Despite not wanting to move out, she knew — given her circumstances — that she mentally couldn't deal with living with her mom any longer.

She felt tears wet her cheeks as she felt her mother envelope her in a hug. She hadn't felt her mother's comforting arms around her body ever since she'd taken up with Jonathan.

All the fear, uncertainty, and disappointment she'd been feeling began tumbling out of her mouth at the same time. "Thank you Mama. Thank you, thank you, thank you," she sobbed. "Thank you for softening your heart. Thank you for your support. Thank you for everything…'cause I'm scared." She shook her head. "Jonathan wants nothing to do with this baby or with me. I...I...I didn't want to go through this on my own."

Betty hugged her daughter even tighter to her bosom and cried right along with her. She was grateful that God had seen fit to put some compassion in her heart for her child. She was glad that the words that her best friend had spoken to her on her situation had finally sunk into her head. "Serenity, you're not alone, honey. You and the baby's got the Lord and you've got me. Just put your hand in his hand, and everything's gonna be alright."

Minutes later, as she was bringing her things back into her childhood bedroom, Serenity couldn't help but fall to her knees at her bedside and begin to pray. "Lord I repent of my sins. In my humble thanks to you...for you showing me your abundant mercy, I'm gonna dedicate my life to you, Lord...and the life of my child to you too. I'll raise my son or daughter up in the right way, heavenly father. No more running around with men...no more playing games. No more letting men use me for their pleasure. I'm dedicating my life to you, Lord. You're all I need. I don't want or need no man in my life."

As she got up from her knees from saying her prayer,

she placed her hand on her still flat belly. For the first time in weeks, she was able to manage a smile. She knew that if she kept her end of the bargain, that the Lord would make things for her and her baby just fine.

*C*HAPTER 3

Six Years Later:

Serenity quickly put the finishing touches on the three dinner plates. Then she shouted out towards the busy servers' station, "Orders up!"

Jared snatched the plates off of the stainless steel, industrial-style restaurant counter. He placed them on his large serving tray using a deftness that had come from several months of experience. Then he flashed the beautiful chef a smile.

"I love it when I'm working shifts with you, Serenity. You make my job easy. You work fast as lightning, but your dishes are delicious — perfectly cooked. I never have to bring an order back...and you *know* that equals a fat tip for *me*."

Without stopping from her work, she chuckled and said, "Thank you, Jay. You know I'd be happy to take ten percent of those tips...right?"

Grinning she shook her head. He was moving so fast towards the restaurant's dining room that her words were directed towards his retreating back. Serenity doubted he'd heard her at all.

Two hours later, as Lucky Rhino Cuisine approached its closing time, Serenity finally had a chance to slow down and breathe. Although the restaurant's owner didn't like any of the employees eating or drinking in the kitchen, she unscrewed the top from her bottle of water and took a quick sip.

"Girl, you know you better not let Mr. Channing see you doing that. He'll probably fly all the way off his rocker this time. You know that man's crazy."

Serenity smiled at her coworker and friend, Chanelle, who also was a chef there at the very popular Greensboro eatery. "Oh, I'm not worried about Mr. Channing tonight. And you shouldn't be either. Deanna said he left for home already — something about a very bad stomach ache."

Chanelle grimaced. "Humph. I wish he could have a very bad stomach ache every night. That way we wouldn't have to deal with him."

Serenity knew it was wrong to wish suffering like that on somebody, but a part of her couldn't help but to agree with Chanelle. Harold Channing was a difficult man to work for. He was a nit-picker — constantly complaining about the work that his employees were doing, even when they were performing their jobs perfectly.

Chanelle took a bite from one of the leftover carrot sticks from the food prep station. "You know we should just up and quit. We should walk out those doors, never to come back...you do know that right?"

Serenity sighed. "Yeah, that would be nice. But personally, I like the pay that I get here. Harold Channing might be a butthole, but he believes in paying people well enough so they'll stick around." She grimaced. "Especially fresh-from-culinary-school graduates like you and me."

Serenity picked up a set of serving utensils. She began placing the leftovers from their work for that day into takeout trays.

Chanelle smiled. "You at it again, girl? Feeding the homeless down the street with Harold Channing's leftovers? I'm sure you remember our butthole of a boss said he didn't want you doing that anymore."

Serenity didn't slow down her pace. She kept piling food onto the plates. Then she frowned. "This food is just gonna be thrown away. I see no reason to place perfectly good meals in the dumpster when someone who's hungry and down on their luck could possibly be filling their belly eating it."

Chanelle sighed. Then she patted her friend on the back. "You got a good heart, Serenity. That's all I'm going to say."

* * *

Ten Minutes Later:

"Here let me get that door for you."

With both her hands full with plastic bags filled with takeout food trays, Serenity smiled at the friendly man who was patiently holding the doors open for her. Then she said, "Thank you."

The stranger grinned in return. "Do you need any help getting everything to your car?"

Serenity shook her head. "Nope. It's not that heavy. I got it...but thanks."

Both of them turned around with puzzled expressions on their faces when a booming voice coming from the street curb got their attention. Serenity's look of puzzlement quickly morphed into a frown.

Jason didn't know why the large, balding man was barreling towards them, cursing with his face turning beet-red in anger, but he could tell that the man seemed to be directing his hostility towards the beautiful girl he'd just opened the door for.

Harold Channing came face to face with Serenity. "What's that in your hands, Serenity?"

Serenity straightened her spine, preparing herself to stand up to her boss. Despite Harold Channing's confrontational behavior, she refused to be intimidated by the man. "These are takeout trays, Mr. Channing."

"Takeout trays? Did you pay for that stuff?"

She shook her head. "No, I didn't. It's the leftovers that were destined for the trash cans out back. I'm taking this food — which is trash to you — to those homeless people around the corner."

Harold placed his lips into a thin, angry line. Then he said, "That's it! I've told you two times that I don't want food from my restaurant going to *those* people. This is the last time you'll pull this little stunt, Serenity...you're fired!"

Serenity looked at the man in disbelief. "Fired?"

"Yes. You can take those bags right back into the kitchen...do it right now. And while you're at it, collect your things. I'll be mailing your final paycheck to you in the morning." He narrowed his beady, blue eyes, "And by the way, Ms. Walker, you're lucky I'm not calling the cops on you for theft. Don't misunderstand me...I'd love to contact the authorities. I just don't want to deal with the hassle!"

"You'd call the police on me for food that you were just going to have the clean-up staff put into the dumpster?"

The man nodded his head. "Yes."

Serenity was seething on the inside. *The nerve of the butthole*, she thought to herself. It was on the tip of her tongue to tell Harold Channing exactly how she felt about him and what he was doing, but right before the words could come out of her mouth, she clamped her lips back shut tight.

As she quietly turned on her heel and made her way back into the restaurant, Serenity knew it had to have been the grace of God himself that had made her hold her peace. She was certain that if she'd said what she'd wanted to to Harold Channing, she would've caught a case.

Chanelle looked up from wiping down the prep station. She frowned when she saw Serenity stride back into the kitchen and plop the bags of takeout on the counter. From the thunderous look on her friend's face, she could tell that something was wrong. "What is it, Serenity? What's done happened?"

Serenity angrily shook her head. "What has

happened Chanelle is I've been fired."

"Fired?!"

"Yeah, you know...fired...canned...axed."

Chanelle followed Serenity's quickly retreating figure to the employee work room. "But I don't understand? You're the best chef here. Why would you be fired?"

"Well—," Serenity said as she hurriedly reached into her locker and took out the few possessions that she always had with her at Lucky Rhino during her workday, "—your wonderful boss was out front when I was coming out with that takeout food for the homeless. Needless to say, he wasn't too pleased about it. He even threatened to have me arrested!"

Chanelle shook her head in utter disbelief. "Arrested!? For taking food he was about to throw in the trash?"

"Yep. You got it."

Chanelle began helping her friend get her things together. "I'm so sorry, Serenity. I know how much you wanted to keep this job. What are you going to do now?"

Serenity didn't know for sure exactly what she was going to do. She frowned then said, "I'm going to pray, then take a number and get back into the unemployment line."

Chanelle let a breath out in a sympathetic sigh. The

she gave Serenity an encouraging little smile. "You're smart and you're a very talented chef. Try not to worry, I'm sure you're going to find a new position. You'll be cooking again, honey...probably quicker than you can even imagine."

As Serenity and Chanelle gave each other hugs goodbye, Serenity couldn't help but frown. Despite what Chanelle had said to try to reassure her, she was worried. As a now-unemployed single mom to a five-year old, how could she not be?

Heavenly father, she thought to herself, *I don't know how you're gonna do it, but it's me again and I need you to turn this situation around. I need you to fix it, Lord.*

* * *

Only minutes later, Serenity walked out of Lucky Rhino Cuisine for what she knew would be the very last time.

She grimaced when she heard the words, "Hi. Judging by your outfit, I assume you're a chef. Based on what I just witnessed out here tonight, I think you're available for employment. I'm opening a restaurant in two months on the other side of town. Here's my card. Give me a call if you're interested in being the executive chef at Heavenly Blue. The pay is very competitive and the job's all yours...that is if you want it."

Chasing Serenity

Serenity watched in amazement as the man who'd opened the door for her earlier that night — the one who had witnessed Harold Channing fire her — walked to his Mercedes Benz and drove away.

As the man's taillights disappeared into the distance, Serenity couldn't help but stare after him with a look of awe, amazement and disbelief written all over her face.

* * *

Jason Bullock guided his vehicle along the highway towards his home on the outskirts of the city. As he took his exit off of the interstate, he couldn't help but think about the girl from back at Lucky Rhino Cuisine.

The curvaceous girl in the chef's get-up had been pretty — gorgeous really — so she'd instantly drawn his attention. But her physical beauty hadn't been what had impressed him and prompted him to offer her employment. It had been the beauty of her soul that had done that. It had been her willingness to go outside of herself to do something worthwhile for another human being — even to the detriment of her own well-being.

He smiled then frowned. "I don't see that type of spirit often," he said to his empty car. "This world needs more of that."

As he made his way into his spacious home, he couldn't help but think to himself, *I hope she decides to give me call and take the job.*

CHAPTER 4

Since she no longer had a job to go to, Serenity decided to use the following morning to brush up her résumé and look for job openings online. She sat down at her kitchen table, right in front of her laptop. Then she sighed. She picked up the business card that the unknown stranger had given her the previous evening, then said, "I guess the first order of business is to give this Jason Bullock person a call."

Minutes later, Serenity placed her phone back down on the table. The man hadn't answered his phone. However, she'd left her name and number on his voicemail and a message that she'd try calling back again later. She frowned.

"Mommy, why you look so sad?"

Serenity instantly turned to her five-year old son, Brayden, and smiled. Her pint-sized dynamo was normally in school on weekday mornings. But since that particular Tuesday was a teacher's workday, he was home with her.

"What do you mean, sweetheart?"

The little boy — who everyone said was the spitting image of his mother — placed his toy truck down on the floor. Then he came and stood by his mother's side. A very serious expression came on his face. "I mean you not happy. You're not smiling like you usually do."

Serenity had no intentions of her current job problems affecting her son's happy-go-lucky spirit. Grinning again to prove her point, she said, "Yes I *am* happy. See."

Little Brayden shook his head. "Nope. Smile's not the same, Mommy. I can tell. I'm pretty smart...'member? Grandma Betty said so."

Serenity couldn't help but pick up her son and start tickling him. As Brayden began laughing, Serenity said, "Pretty smart you say...is that right?"

"Yep. Handsome, too."

Serenity chuckled. "Let me guess....Grandma Betty said so? She said you're handsome, too?"

Still giggling, the little boy nodded his head. "Mm hm."

"Well, okay then, my little handsome smartypants...go get your shoes on. Just like I promised you, we're going out this morning to get you new crayons and paints."

"A new coloring book too, Mommy?"

Serenity smiled. "Sure baby. A new coloring book as well."

* * *

By the time they made it back home, it was a little past the lunch hour. Seeing that Serenity knew her son was anxious to get started on using his newly purchased art supplies, she left him in his bedroom at his kiddie table while she went back into the kitchen.

Since she'd accidentally left her cellphone at home, she couldn't stop herself from wondering if she'd received a call from Jason Bullock in regards to his job offer. A quick check of her cellphone showed that besides a call from Chanelle, she hadn't missed a thing.

She let a breath out on a sigh and booted up her laptop. "I guess it's time to get started on some online job applications," she said softly under her breath.

Two hours later, Serenity knew she was in trouble. She'd checked all the hiring websites — the ones she'd bookmarked from the last time she'd job hunted — but no one was seeking to fill a chef's position. She frowned. *Not even a prep chef.*

She leaned back and shook her head in disappointment. Then she pulled out a notepad and a pencil. Twenty minutes later, after a full sheet's worth of calculations, she came to a sad realization — without employment, the money in her checking and savings accounts would only last her and Brayden two months.

"I'm all done coloring, Mommy. May I have a sandwich and juice please?"

Normally aware of every little sound Brayden would make, Serenity had been so engrossed in her problem that she hadn't even heard her son pad into the room.

Not wanting a repeat of what had happened that morning when her child had asked her why she was so sad, Serenity quickly pasted a cheery smile on her face. "Of course, son...you may have a sandwich and a glass of juice. Just give mommy a minute and I'll put it right here on the table."

As she watched her son eating his lunch, Serenity had to wonder if their little twenty dollar shopping spree that morning had been a wise idea. Twenty dollars wasn't a lot of money. However, with her lack of viable job prospects, she knew it was time to hold on to every dollar to her name...*hold on to it with an iron-closed fist.*

* * *

Chasing Serenity

A Month Later:

This is not where I thought I'd be with a four-year culinary arts degree. That's what Serenity thought to herself. Then she frowned.

"Serenity, we're not paying you overtime. You need to go ahead and clock out."

She wiped her hands down the front of her fast food uniform and prepared to leave the kitchen. Working as a fry cook at Burger Galaxy was a far cry from being an executive chef — like she'd been at Lucky Rhino Cuisine. But it was better than the alternative — which would have been making no money at all.

"Remember," Serenity's manager said to her. "I don't have you on the schedule coming in again until Monday."

"Monday, Mr. Brown? But I need at least ten more hours this week."

The man shook his head. "I'm sorry. That's all I've got for you."

She knew that saying anything else on the matter was pointless. *If that's all he says he got, then that's all there is to it.*

Five minutes later, as she was making her way out of Burger Galaxy, she couldn't stop the frown that instantly appeared on her face. *There he is — Jason Bullock — the very same Jason Bullock who'd promised me that job.*

"You know I tried calling you using that number on your card. I left several messages saying that I wanted the position. Even if you'd changed your mind about hiring me, the least you could have done was to have let me know."

Under normal circumstances, she wouldn't probably have said anything to the man at all. But after a ten-hour monotonous shift at Burger Galaxy, flipping beef patties and cooking fries, her irritation was a little difficult to control.

Jason's first instinct was to grin when he noticed who was talking to him. But seeing the look on her beautiful face, that grin quickly morphed into a frown. "I'm sorry Ms. — um," he grinned, "—I just realized that I don't even know your name."

Since she wanted to hear exactly what the man had to say — what lame excuse he was going to come up with — she said, "Ms. Walker. You can call me Ms. Walker."

He nodded his head. "Ms. Walker, I'm sorry. I didn't get any of your messages."

Serenity frowned. "Well, I don't know how that could be the case. I called the number that you gave me."

As proof she dug into her purse. "Here's your card."

At that point, Jason frowned. "This is my old number...my old card. I thought I had thrown all of these away. Ms. Walker...I'm so sorry."

She nodded her head, and said, "Yeah. Sure you are."

"Do you still want the position? I have three chef slots — one is still open. I was trying to wait until the last minute to fill it. I was kinda hoping you'd call."

She looked at him with doubt in her eyes. "You don't even know if I can really cook or not. Why would I assume that you're telling me the truth? That you're saving a spot for me? That you even *have* a restaurant that you're opening."

He smiled. "Construction will be completed on my restaurant tomorrow — by the way it's called Heavenly Blue. The head contractor is there as we speak. We can go over and you can ask him questions about my ownership of the place if you'd like. As for your other question — you know the one about my confidence in your cooking skills. Well Ms. Walker, your old boss — Harold Channing — the man may be a butthole, but his restaurant is an upscale establishment. One that is very successful. I'm pretty much sure you wouldn't have been cooking for him unless you were good at what you do."

His explanation had made a lot of sense, but she still wasn't convinced on his sincerity. "And you'd just hire me out of the blue...just like that? No references or nothing?"

At that he grinned again. "Yes, as a matter of fact I would. Anybody who'd put their own well-being on the line like you did that night — you know, trying to do the right thing and give that food to the homeless — anybody like that would receive five gold stars in my book."

He knew that working at Burger Galaxy had probably come with a significant cut in her salary. And since he'd heard her only minutes earlier asking her boss for overtime, he kind of suspected that she could use some extra funds. Therefore, he smiled and said, "If you want to — and for the inconvenience that I caused by giving you incorrect contact information — we can go to my bank today and I can pay you for your first month in advance...as well as a sign-on bonus."

Seeing that it had taken her a month to find employment at Burger Galaxy, and that her current position only paid one-third of what her job at Lucky Rhino had, things were pretty tight financially for her at that particular time in her life.

The faintest hint of a smile appeared on her lips.

"Okay Mr. Bullock. I believe you've managed to win me over. I think I'd like to take you up on your offer. But—", she hesitated for the briefest of moments then continued speaking, "—I'd need an official contract of employment from you first."

Pleased with her response, he grinned. He nodded his head. "Sure, Ms. Walker. Of course."

* * *

The following morning, Serenity sat in the newly-built, beautiful building that housed Heavenly Blue International Cuisine. She was staring at the employment contract that Jason Bullock had just handed her. The salary that he was offering was double what she'd been receiving at Lucky Rhino. And the bonus would cover all of her bills for an entire month.

"Is there a problem, Ms. Walker?"

Serenity shook her head. "No." She picked up the ink pen from the table. "No problem at all."

"I know you have to give the people at Burger Galaxy some type of official resignation. Will you be able to start work for me in a week?"

Serenity nodded her head. "I believe I can make that happen, Mr. Bullock."

Chasing Serenity

As she drove away in her late model Toyota Camry with the check he'd given her nestled in her glove box, she had a Kool-Aid grin on her pretty face. She knew it was nothing but the grace of God that had allowed her to land the job.

CHAPTER 5

"You got offered a job where?"

Serenity curled her feet under herself on her sofa. "At Heavenly Blue. It's the new restaurant that was just built over off of Friendly Avenue."

Jasmine looked over at her best friend while wearing a puzzled expression on her pretty cocoa-brown face. "Um...Heavenly Blue. That name sounds familiar for some reason." Then she snapped her fingers together. She smiled. "Oh now I remember. I saw a segment about that restaurant coming to town last month on News 2. It's being opened by the football player — Jason Bullock."

Then Jasmine shrugged her shoulders. "Well ex-football player that is. He played for the Charlotte Cardinals. He was sidelined by a really bad knee injury a few years ago. Hasn't gone back to balling since."

Serenity didn't follow sports at all, so there was no way that she would have known who he was. Needless to say, she was shocked. Not to mention wondering why a football player — *well, ex-football player*, she thought to herself — would want to even open up a restaurant.

An excited grin worked its way across Jasmine's face. "Girl, you said you actually got to meet him in person?!"

Serenity nodded her head. She smiled. "Uh yeah. Like I said, he's my new boss. He offered me the job personally."

"Wow! You are so lucky, Serenity. Girl, I wish my boss was a hottie like Jason Bullock." She began fanning herself with her hand for emphasis.

Serenity frowned. Then she smiled. "You know, Jasmine. I didn't even notice him in that way. He's just another guy to me."

Then it was Jasmine's turn to grimace. "I bet you didn't notice him, Serenity. That's 'cause honey, you stopped noticing men ever since you hooked up with Brayden's butthole of a daddy. I think it's well past time for you to get back out there on the dating scene." She shook her head. "Or at least give yourself permission to notice that a good-looking man like Jason Bullock is in your presence." Then she chuckled. "Like my mama said — it don't hurt to look."

"Girl, you know I love her, but your mama is a mess."

Then Serenity sighed. She shrugged her shoulders. "Brayden is my life now. He's who I'm focused on. He already has zero relationship with his daddy — since Jonathan doesn't want to see him at all." She shook her head. "I can't drag different men in my son's life every week...confusing him, messing him up."

"Nobody's asking you to drag different men in Brayden's life, Serenity. You know there's a such thing as just going out on a date...right? Going out on dates don't necessarily equate to bringing random guys to your home and introducing them to your son. Plus, single mothers date all the time — even saved ones like yourself."

Then Jasmine pointed her finger at Serenity. "Haven't you heard of that dating website ChristianSingleParentsMeet.com? I know you have. Their commercial says that they have hundreds of thousands of members. That means that plenty of you God-fearing unattached mothers out there not only believe in dating, but are actually doing it."

At that point, Serenity stood up from her sofa. She reached her hands above her head and yawned. Then she laughed. "Um...does the commercial also mention the male to female ratio for their website? I bet there are five hundred and two thousand members who are men, but only twenty-three who are women."

Jasmine shook her head. "You know I have half the mind to sign you up. But I bet you wouldn't even give whatever poor guy who happened to be interested in you a chance."

Serenity smiled at Jasmine sweetly. Then she laughed again. "At least I know my bestfriend knows me well. Girl, you just hit the nail right on the head. That's exactly what I'd do."

* * *

Later on that night, after Jasmine had gone home, Serenity laid back in her bed and closed her eyes. She began thinking back over everything she and Jasmine had talked about that evening. For the first time since giving birth to her son, she realized that she was lonely. That she had some type of void in her heart that was going unfilled.

Then she sat back up in bed wearing a surprised frown on her face. "Dang...Jasmine is right. Jason Bullock is fine."

She shook her head in dismay. She was disappointed in herself for spontaneously thinking about the man in that manner.

She laid back down, pulled her covers up to her chin, then closed her eyes. Even with her eyes closed she was having a hard time banishing away the image imprinted in her brain of the man's smiling face.

She sighed. "I don't need to be worrying about how handsome my boss is. Take these thoughts away, Jesus. Lord, please just take 'em away."

* * *

Across Town:

Jason pulled back his sheets and plopped down on his king-sized bed. He laced his fingers together and placed them behind his head. Then he smiled. He'd almost ruined successfully getting Serenity Walker to work for him. But at the last minute, God had shown up and corrected his rookie mistake. In retrospect, he couldn't believe that he'd actually handed her one of his old cards that evening almost a month ago.

He shook his head at his error, then he grinned again. He had a really good feeling about hiring Serenity. He was sure she'd get along with the rest of his staff. He was positive that she'd be a good asset to his team. But there was another reason he was happy that he'd hired her. However, he just couldn't seem to put his finger on it.

An unbidden image of her smiling face suddenly popped into his mind. She was a breathtakingly beautiful woman. But he'd seen plenty of lovely girls in his thirty-five years on Earth. So he was sure her looks wasn't part of the reason he was happy he'd signed her on.

Deciding not to think too hard on the situation, he reached over and turned off his bedside lamp. *I'm sure I'll figure it out at a later time.*

$\mathcal{C}$HAPTER 6

The restaurant's grand opening wasn't slated for another week, but Serenity was certain that she was going to enjoy working at Heavenly Blue. Her new boss had introduced her to her coworkers and she liked all of them. The entire work team, from the waitstaff to the chefs — all of whom Jason Bullock had dubbed 'The Blue Crew' — were easy for her to get along with.

"Now tell me, Serenity....what do you think of the menu offerings?"

Jason had just called her into his office. He'd said he had something that he'd wanted to speak to her about in private.

Sitting across the desk from him, she said, "I like it."

He nodded his head. "Yes, it's a nice menu. Carl, Evan and I came up with it ourselves. But what I really want to know, is what do you *really* think of it. Be open, be honest...you won't hurt my feelings." Then he chuckled.

She had to admit, there were a few changes that she'd noticed that she would have implemented if Heavenly Blue had been her restaurant. *Or if I were the master chef*, she thought to herself. *But the master chef is Carl's position and I'd never step on his toes.*

At that point, Jason chuckled again. "And by the way, neither will Carl. I mean Carl won't be offended by your suggestions." He made a quick encouraging gesture with his hand. "Go ahead, Serenity...speak your mind."

"Well...Mr. Bullock. There *is* a thing or two."

From his positive responses to her two suggestions, the 'thing or two' that she'd initially told him she'd change...well, it quickly turned into seven things.

Smiling, he nodded his head. "I think you've come up with some great ideas, Serenity. I'm sure Carl will agree with me. Carl is a seasoned chef, but sometimes a fresh perspective from someone younger can make a world of a difference in a thing."

Her previous boss — Harold Channing — would have never said anything of the sort to her. In fact, with her only holding the role of junior chef at Lucky Rhino Cuisine, the man would've never asked her opinion anyway. Needless to say, Jason Bullock had just made her feel like she was a valued employee — an esteemed member of the Heavenly Blue team. She'd never experienced that at any other job she'd held.

He looked at her with a curious expression on his face. "What is it, Serenity? What's wrong?"

She smiled. She shook her head. "Oh, nothing really, Mr. Bullock. I guess it just feels good to be working someplace where I feel appreciated."

He understood completely. He nodded his head. "Point taken, Serenity. And by the way, I'd appreciate it if you just called me Jason...we're all on a first name basis around here."

She didn't reply right away so he said, "You're not comfortable calling me by my first name? You don't like it?" He chuckled, thinking of something that his younger sister had told him years ago when they'd both been teenagers. "It reminds you of the slasher from the horror movie series Friday 13th or something?"

"Actually, no...I think Jason is a perfectly fine name." She grinned. "I'm not into horror flicks, but I suspect you are."

She was surprised when a somewhat sad look came over his features. He sighed. "Nope, but my little sister was."

She gave him a tentative smile. "It must be nice having a sibling. I'm an only child myself, but I've always wished that I had a sister or a brother."

Apparently over his brief moment of sadness, he returned her grin with one of his own. Then he laughed. "I have five of them — siblings that is — maybe I can give you one as a loaner."

She couldn't help but chuckle a little. "I'm sure your sisters and brothers wouldn't be too happy to hear you saying that."

Lovingly thinking of his family members, he nodded his head in agreement. "No. I'm pretty much sure they wouldn't."

"Well, Mr. Bullock...um, I mean Jason, I think I'd better get back into the kitchen. Carl and Evan are waiting on me. We're supposed to be doing a dry run of the specials that we're offering for opening night."

A full minute after she'd left his office, Jason was still wearing a smile on his face. Besides his siblings, he hadn't felt so comfortable talking to someone in a very long time. For some reason, to him it felt like he'd known Serenity forever. He wasn't quite sure what to think of that. But he did know that he liked the feeling.

* * *

"Touchdown...we nailed it you guys!"

It was the end of their opening night and the last

customer had just left Heavenly Blue International Cuisine.

Jason grinned as all fourteen of his employees stood in a semicircle around him. "Yep...we nailed it and I want to thank each and every one of you for making our opening night an overwhelming success! As a token of my appreciation, everybody's gonna be seeing bonuses in their paychecks this week. You all worked hard...you deserve it!"

Serenity couldn't help but grin and clap her hands in response to Jason's little announcement, just like the rest of her coworkers.

Jason's semi-celebrity status as a pro ex-football player had assured that Heavenly Blue had had plenty of media coverage prior to the opening. Consequently, the house had been packed and the patrons had all appeared to have enjoyed their food. The local newspaper's food critic had even promised Jason that he'd have a glowing review in the paper's upcoming Sunday edition.

Since Jason had decided to include a clean-up crew as part of his restaurant's operation, Serenity and the other two chef's didn't have to stay after hours to tidy up.

As soon as Jason had finished his announcements, Serenity made her way to the employee room to prepare herself to leave for the evening. As she was hanging up her chef's coat in her locker, she was surprised to hear Jason say behind her, "That was a good call that you made on the dessert, Serenity. The banana pudding souffle with butter-rum sauce was a hit. You killed it."

Serenity couldn't stop the pleased smile that made its way on her face from his complement. The recipe had been one that she'd created herself. "You think they liked it?"

He nodded his head. "I'm sure of it. At least three people asked for the recipe." He winked his eye at her then continued speaking. "I, of course had to tell them that it's my star chef's trade secret. I'm happy the governor's wife understood."

"The first lady of our state ate my food?"

He grinned. "Yep. Her son and I played ball together at Duke. She was happy to come out tonight and show her support."

She pulled her raincoat out of the locker and began putting it on. She was surprised when Jason closed the short distance between them and said, "Here...let me help you with that."

She allowed him to help her into her rainslicker and then she picked up her umbrella.

Jason smiled. "It's only a short walk from the restaurant's front doors to the parking lot. With all that get-up, a person would think that you're preparing yourself to take a long, solitary trek in the pouring rain."

She grimaced. "That's because I am." Then she smiled. "Well at least a walk to the bus stop on the corner down the street."

He was confused. "I thought you drove to work this morning. I saw your car out front."

She nodded her head. "I did. But it died on me as soon as I'd made my way into the parking lot. I had to call a wrecker earlier this afternoon and have it towed."

"You don't have to take the bus. I'm on my way out of here, too. I'll drop you off along the way."

She gave him a look that was full of skepticism, then she laughed. "That's alright, boss. I mean Jason. From what I understand, you live in the 'burbs outside of town. I live on the south side. There's no way that my apartment is '*along the way*' as you said. It's more like waaaay out of your way — opposite directions really."

Grinning, he shook his head. "Oh, no worries, Serenity. I absolutely can't let my favorite chef walk home in the rain after our fabulous opening night."

"Favorite chef? Really?" She laughed, not even believing him one bit. "It's a good thing that Carl and Evan have already left for the evening. I wonder what they'd say if they heard you calling me your '*favorite*'."

He chuckled right along with her. "I'll just tell them that I was mesmerized by your beautiful smile. They're guys. They'll understand that."

She knew he was in no way being serious, but nevertheless, his comment threw her for a loop.

It took him only a few seconds to realize that some of the happy-go-lucky camaraderie between them had suddenly disappeared.

He gave her a tiny smile. "For some reason, Serenity Walker, I think I'm always putting my foot in my mouth when it comes to you. What did I say wrong?"

She shook her head. "Oh...it was nothing. I suddenly got tired I guess."

"You sure?"

"Yep. Positive."

He wasn't quite certain that he completely believed her, but he sensed that it would be in his best interest to not press the issue. Therefore he simply said, "Give me a few minutes to get my things and I'll be ready to go."

* * *

A slow smile settled on Serenity's lips when he brought his extended cab truck to a smooth stop outside of her apartment complex. "It's a good thing my son isn't out here to see you bring me home. He would be insisting on a ride."

"You have a son?" he asked her in surprise.

She nodded her head. "Yes. I do."

He couldn't help but wonder if she had a husband that came along with her son. He hadn't seen a ring on her finger. But seeing that she was a professional chef, that wouldn't have been too unusual. A lot of chefs that he'd run into didn't wear jewelry on their hands due to food safety concerns.

"Your husband isn't the jealous type is he? He won't be mad that I drove you home?"

She shook her head. "Nope. He won't be mad at all."

For some reason, he felt disappointed that she had a husband. *But in all honesty, I should've expected it*, he thought to himself. *After all, the good ones are always taken — not that it really matters to me, of course. I'm done playing the dating game.*

Then he smiled when she continued speaking.

"My husband won't be mad, because I don't have one. It's just me and my son, Brayden. He's five and really into trucks right now for some reason." Thinking about her kid, she grinned. "The bigger the truck, the better to him."

"Oh, my son's the same way. In fact, I'm taking him

to a monster truck show this weekend. He's five...just like your Brayden. His name's Tyson, by the way."

She nodded her head. She smiled. "Ummm...I bet your wife isn't looking forward to that little outing. Even though I've been thinking about taking Brayden to one of the shows, I hear they're loud and a little bit boisterous."

"Oh, I'm not married, Serenity. I'm a single dad. It's just Tyson and me—," then he smiled, "—and a host of aunties and uncles...all mixed in with a couple of grandparents."

She looked at him in puzzlement. "I never would have figured you for a single dad. How in the world did that happen?" Then she quickly added, "That is if you don't mind me asking, of course."

He fixed his gaze on the front window of his truck, not looking at anything in particular. He sighed. "I would have imagined that you'd read about it in the tabloids — pro Cardinals quarterback, Jason Bullock, permanently sidelined with knee injury. Wife doesn't appreciate the drastic drop in his income. She consequently leaves him and his infant son. Divorces him and marries his uninjured teammate. End of story."

Serenity frowned. "I don't follow the tabloids, Jason. I believe their mostly trash." She instinctively reached over and covered his hand with her own. She gave it a gentle squeeze of empathy. "I'm so sorry you had to go through that."

He appreciated her empathy and he had to admit to himself that her holding his hand felt normal. It felt natural. Like they'd been holding hands off and on in that fashion for a lifetime.

He gave her a tiny smile. "Thank you for your heartfelt compassion, Serenity."

She returned his smile with one of her own and slowly placed her hand back into her lap. She really did feel bad for her boss. His wife leaving not only him, but also their child, because the millions had dried up wasn't right. "You're welcome, Jason."

They were quiet for several seconds. Then he said, "I actually have two extra tickets to the monster truck show this weekend. I can let you have them if you'd like. My brother and his son were supposed to go to the event with me and Tyson. But my nephew came down with the flu yesterday, so we're pretty much sure they won't be going. It's just gonna be Tyson and me. The other two tickets would be going to waste."

Serenity frowned. "I believe I heard on the news that the show you're talking about is an hour's drive away from here. As much as I'd love to take you up on your offer — for Brayden's sake of course — I'm gonna have to say no. My car won't be out of the shop until late tomorrow afternoon...maybe even early evening."

He was quick with his response. "I'd be happy to pick the two of you up. We could go together. That is if you're game." Grinning, he shrugged his shoulders. "It's the least I can do for my favorite chef and her son."

She smiled at the '*favorite chef*' part of his comment. Then she thought about his offer for several seconds. Due to her financial hardships over the past couple of months, things had been a little rough on her son — *no matter how hard I tried to make it so that he wouldn't know there was a financial problem.*

She sighed inwardly. *Brayden deserves an experience like this*, she thought to herself. *He would enjoy it.*

She gave Jason a smile. "It's a good thing my boss gave me tomorrow off from Heavenly Blue. I guess I'll take you up on your offer."

"Can I pick you up here at eight-thirty? We can do breakfast on the road along the way?"

"Sure. Why not?"

CHAPTER 7

"It is not a date, Jasmine."

"Uh, sweetie. I beg to differ."

Serenity sighed into her cellphone. As soon as she'd gotten into her apartment, paid her babysitter, and sent the super-dependable seventeen year old home, her cellphone had begun to ring. It of course had been Jasmine calling to check on how things had gone at the restaurant's opening.

Serenity shook her head. "Like I told you, Jasmine...Jason had a couple of extra tickets that he didn't want to see go to waste."

Jasmine giggled. "Oh, I see...you guys are suddenly on a first name basis now. You're calling your boss '*Jason*', but it's not a date."

Serenity shook her head. "I don't know what I'm gonna do with you, Jasmine. I'm calling him '*Jason*' because he asked me to call him that. He wants *all* of his employees to call him that. It doesn't mean that I'm special or something...and it certainly isn't proof that we're going on a date."

Smiling into the phone, Jasmine said, "Alright, honey. I'll just let you have your delusions this time. But remember, you're not fooling me one bit." Then she laughed. "I'll see you in church on Sunday, Serenity. I have to get some rest. I have an early day tomorrow."

After she'd disconnected her call with Jasmine, Serenity looked at herself in her bedroom mirror. Then she began speaking to her reflection. "Jasmine is wrong. It's definitely *not* a date."

* * *

The Next Morning:

Jason glanced into his rearview mirror at the two boys seated side-by-side in booster seats giggling. Then he smiled and looked at the woman in his passenger-side seat. "Our boys like each other. They're like two peas in a pod."

Serenity nodded her head. She couldn't agree more. She'd had reservations about her son getting along with Jason's child because she knew Brayden was a normally reserved little person — meaning, it usually took him a while to warm up to other people. But as soon as her son had met both Jason and Tyson, he'd lit up like a light bulb.

She smiled. "I think it's their common love of trucks."

Looking back at their boys, who'd each brought their favorite toy truck along for the ride, he grinned and nodded his head. "I think, Serenity, that I agree."

Then he chuckled. "And what about their parents? What about us? Are we like two peas in a pod, too?"

She knew that he was joking. But some reason, his question had made her wonder what it would be like if they were on a real date. She quickly pushed that thought from her mind and said, "Um, we've known each other all of three weeks. I'd highly doubt that."

True they'd only known each other for three weeks, but to Jason, it felt like he'd known Serenity forever. With his eyes focused on the highway, a gentle smile worked its way across his lips. "Have you ever met someone new, but you felt like you'd known that person all your life? Like maybe you were together in another lifetime or something"

She shook her head. She laughed. "Since I don't believe in reincarnation, I can't honestly say that I have."

He put on his blinker and turned into the pavilion that was hosting the event then said, "Neither do I — I mean I don't believe in reincarnation — but for some reason I kind of get that feeling about you."

Serenity was happy that the boys had noticed they'd arrived at their destination and had begun shouting in excitement. Why? Because she didn't know exactly how to respond to what her boss had just said to her.

Jason grinned at the boys in the back seat of his truck. Then he caught both sets of their eyes in his rearview mirror. He chuckled. "Calm down, you two. They'll never let us through the front gates if you're making that much noise."

Serenity couldn't help but smile at how Brayden and Tyson both instantly toned down their excitement. Then to Jason she said, "Wow, I think I'm gonna have to steal some of your parenting tips."

"Oh, for you Serenity Walker, my parenting tips are absolutely free." He shrugged his shoulders. "Not that I think you need parenting tips from me. You've done an excellent job with Brayden. Your parenting skills really shine through him."

Serenity would be lying if she'd said she wasn't pleased by his statement. She smiled. "Thank you, Jason. I think you've done a great job with Tyson, too."

He brought the car to a stop in a parking slot. "Well, thank you. However, I can't take all the credit for that.

When it comes to raising Tyson, I've had plenty of help from my mom. I don't think I would have made it through those first few months if I hadn't had her and the Lord on my side."

Serenity nodded her head. She understood exactly where he was coming from. In fact, she felt the exact same way about her mom...about God, too. If it hadn't been for the both of them, she wasn't sure exactly where she and her son would have ended up at in life.

As the boys began to get a little antsy in the back seat, he grinned across at Serenity. "I think we'd better go ahead and get these two into the building. I'm not exactly sure how long the effects of those good parenting skills that you say I have are gonna last."

Taking a quick glance at their boys herself, she smiled. She couldn't agree more.

* * *

The show was an absolute hit with both Tyson and Brayden. Serenity had been expecting that. However, she had to admit to herself that she'd enjoyed the event as well. That part had come as a complete surprise to her.

With all four of them holding hands — the two kids were located in the middle of Serenity and Jason — they all walked out of the special events center.

As Jason helped the boys into their booster seats, he grinned. "The show wasn't that great was it fellas?"

Serenity wasn't surprised to see both boys shaking their heads in disagreement and talking over each other about just how awesome the monster truck event had been.

Seconds later, when he'd finally settled himself into the driver's seat, Jason looked over at Serenity. He was wearing a grin on his face. "Bet you thought you weren't gonna have a good time."

She returned his smile with one of her own. "I had a great time today, Jason. What would make you say that?"

He pointed to her oversized purse. Then he laughed. "Most people don't pack a small library of their favorite books and mags if they think they're going someplace that's interesting to them...someplace they think they're gonna have a good time. You came like you were prepared to fight off boredom."

"How do you know that I don't carry a few books and mags around with me all the time, Jason Bullock?"

"Because, Serenity...I've seen you come to work at Heavenly Blue. Remember? It always amazes me just how much you can stuff into that tiny purse that you bring everyday." Then he laughed.

She didn't even bother to reply to his last statement. She knew that she was busted — that the gig was up. She smiled instead.

Seeing the look of amused defeat in her dark brown eyes, he couldn't help but chuckle again. "I called it didn't I? Am I right or am I right?"

"Okay, okay. I admit that I didn't think I'd enjoy the show as much as I did. Thank you for inviting Brayden and I to tag along."

"You're welcome. We're going to the children's museum next weekend. Think you might be interested?"

"Science museum?! Say yes, mommy! Please say yes!"

Serenity turned in her seat to look at her son and Tyson. Tyson flashed his dad's new friend a winning smile. Then he said, "Please say yes, Ms. Serenity. Me and Brayden will have big, big, big fun!" He'd stretched his little arms out wide to emphasize just how great of a time he thought him and Brayden would have together.

Jason's son, Tyson, was a total cutie-pie. Between his and her own child's urgings, she wasn't exactly surprised to hear herself say, "Okay, you two. I think you've managed to convince me. My answer is yes."

Jason chuckled. Then he leaned over in his seat and whispered to Serenity, "I forgot to warn you that my son is a pint-sized charmer. He has both of his grandparents and all of his aunties and uncles wrapped around his little pinky finger."

Thinking about how her boss had somehow managed to convince her to come along with him and his son that very day, she grinned. Then she shook her head. "Mmmm...I wonder who he gets his 'charming-folks' skills from?"

With his eyes on the road, but with a smile on his face, he said, "So you think I'm charming?"

She shook her head. "I didn't say that. It's more like you're a *charmer*."

He smiled. "Charmer...charming...is there a real difference?"

"Yes. And you know there is." She grinned. "If we didn't have kids in the car, I'd explain it to you. In fact, I'll probably explain to you at a later date."

"Can I hold you to it?"

Wait a second...is he flirting with me? That was the thought that had suddenly rushed through her head. Then she just as quickly corrected her thinking. *Of course he's not. I'm getting as bad as Jasmine, now. Pretty soon, I'm gonna be assuming that we're on a real date.*

"Serenity...did you hear me?"

"Huh? What?"

He grinned. "Where did you go to just now? I must not be but too much of a charmer...I can't even seem to hold your attention with my conversation."

Oh, you had my attention alright. You don't even know how much so. But of course she couldn't say that out loud. So instead she said, "Oh, I'm sorry. I think I must be getting tired. I'm almost just as bad as those two peas in the pod — you know...the ones who are now asleep in your back seat."

He took a quick glance in his rearview mirror. Then he chuckled. "I was wondering why it had gotten so quiet."

"Yeah. I know right?"

Then she sighed. "I wonder how Carl, Evan and the crew are doing at Heavenly Blue?"

"Oh, they're doing just fine. I called in to check on things a couple of times this evening. Business is still booming." He smiled. "I'm very satisfied."

She nodded her head. "Not to get all up into your business, but tonight is only the second night Heavenly Blue has been open. It would seem to me that you would have wanted to hang around there a little longer...you know, bask in the grand opening limelight?"

He smiled. "Yeah. You're right. I wanted to be at Heavenly Blue, but I promised Tyson months ago that

I'd take him to the monster truck event. My son always comes first, Serenity. Taking off today was a sacrifice for me." He let out a breath in a contented sigh. "But seeing the smile on my son's face today made it all well worth it."

She was impressed by his very apparent commitment as a father. She shared with him as much.

"I appreciate you noticing my effort to be a great dad to Tyson. But I really can't imagine myself *not* trying to be a good parent. I love my son and I'm the only parent that he has. I have to try twice as hard...you know, try to make it so that he's not missing his mother's presence in his life."

Serenity was curious. She wanted to ask him more about his ex, but she decided that it would be somewhat inappropriate — seeing that they didn't have that type of relationship. Instead, she simply nodded her head and said, "I understand, Jason. I'm the same way with Brayden. I work extra hard on parenting in hopes that he won't miss the father who's chosen not to play a role in his life."

They spent the next thirty minutes in companionable silence, each absorbed in their own thoughts.

When Jason brought his truck to a smooth stop outside of her apartment complex, he turned to Serenity and smiled. "Thank you for a wonderful day, Serenity. I'll let you in on a little secret...I love spending time with my son, but I don't think it would have been as fun for me today without you tagging along." She was surprised when he reached over, covered her hand with his own and gave it a little squeeze. "You're good company. Thank you for coming."

She suddenly felt shy. Working past the frog that seemed stuck in her throat, her eyes met his in the semi-darkness of the truck's interior. "You're...you're welcome. I had a great time, too. Thank you for inviting me...I mean us."

Brayden chose that moment to stir in the back seat. "We home, mommy?"

She slowly pulled her hand out of Jason's. "Yes we are, son."

Jason grinned. "I'll help you two get to the front door."

Serenity shook her head. "My front door's only a few yards away from this truck. I can manage."

Now it was his turn to shake his head in disagreement. "A real gentleman never let's a lady walk herself to her front door after a night out on the town."

She didn't necessarily consider their outing to be a night out on the town — especially with their two boys tagging along — but she chose not to argue the point with him. She decided to just let him carry the booster seat and Brayden to her front door.

Later on that night, after Serenity had said her prayers, her mind couldn't seem stop itself from settling on thoughts about Jason. She smiled when she thought about the pleasant day they'd shared together. "Jasmine is right," she said to her empty bedroom. "Jason Bullock really *is* a hottie."

She shook her head, then frowned at her statement. "Where in the world did that comment come from, Lord? He's my boss. He's just trying to be nice to me. I shouldn't be thinking about the man in that way."

She pursed her lips into a thin line of disapproval and shook her head again. "Some of Jasmine must be rubbing off on me. She's always talking to me about herself dating this guy and that one. That must be what all of this is about."

She nodded her head, pleased with the rationale she'd come up with to explain away what she considered to be completely errant notions.

She quickly turned off her lamp and settled under the covers. Before sleep finally claimed her for the night, her last thought was, *Plus I'm not into dating. I've dedicated my life to my Lord and Savior and to my son. I don't have time for a man in my life. Not now, not later...not anytime. And if on the off chance I somehow changed my mind, I definitely wouldn't go out with my boss.*

$\mathcal{C}$HAPTER 8

"Your daddy did what?"

Bryan Bullock looked across the breakfast table at his five year old nephew, Tyson, as he'd asked the little boy the question. They were all having bacon, eggs, and toast together, seeing that it was the Bullock family tradition to get together and have breakfast as a family on the first Sunday morning of the month — right before church.

At least seven pairs of adult eyes turned to look at the little boy. They were all his aunts and uncles, as well as his grandparents.

"I said Daddy took me on the date that he had last night with Ms. Serenity. I got to meet her little boy. His name's Brayden. I like them. Ms. Serenity is nice and Brayden likes trucks...just like me. We're going to the children's museum next weekend. All four of us."

Jason wanted to crawl under the table at that point. He loved his family dearly. However, he was bone-tired and he wasn't up for playing twenty-four questions that morning. *Especially after I kept waking up last night from dream after dream about Serenity.*

"You're finally dating again, Jason?" His brother, Paul, who was sitting next to him patted him on the back. "I'm proud of you, bro."

With a smile on her face, his mother chimed in too. "Thank you, Jesus! It's about time." After her little hallelujah praise break, she grinned at her youngest son and said, "When do the rest of us get to meet her? She must be pretty special if you allowed her to meet Tyson. I know you wouldn't allow just anybody into your son's life."

Jason shook his head. "No, no, no, no...Tyson got it all wrong."

Mrs. Bullock was confused. "What did he get all wrong, son?"

"Serenity...I mean Ms. Walker and I aren't dating. She's one of the new chef's that I hired at Heavenly Blue."

His very single older brother, Micah, was the first to reply to that. "You mean the gorgeous knockout that was burning it up in the kitchen at Heavenly Blue on your premiere night? The one with the smouldering eyes and the curves in all the right places."

Mrs. Bullock gave her son a slap on the arm. With a stern look in her eyes she said, "Watch your mouth, Micah. We have kids at the table you know."

Mr. Bullock, the patriarch of the family, backed his wife up with, "That's right, boy."

Immediately contrite, Micah apologized to both his parents. But the look of appreciation that he had in his eyes for his brother's newest hiree didn't go anywhere. He turned to Jason. "Is she who you didn't take out last night? The beautiful chef at Heavenly Blue?"

For some reason, Jason didn't like the very appreciative way that his brother was thinking about Serenity. He frowned.

Thomas Bullock gave his son a stern look. "Now leave your brother alone, Micah. If he says he's not dating, then he's not dating."

A frown came across Tyson's face. He didn't understand and he was worried. "But you, me, Brayden, and Ms. Serenity...we still going to the children's museum, right dad?"

Jason gave his son a smile. Overlooking everything his family would probably think from his comment he said, "We sure are, sport."

Sensing that her son didn't want to speak on the subject anymore, Henrietta Bullock changed their discussion line over to the weather. But not before thinking to herself, *Guess I'll have to get to the bottom of this Serenity Walker business at a later time.* She smiled to herself. *If I'm lucky, maybe even after church today.*

Jason felt like he'd dodged a bullet. If he and Serenity were indeed dating, his family would have been the first people to know about it. That's just how tight of a bond they all shared. However, since she was only his employee and not his girlfriend, he didn't need his family having false speculations about her. *Plus*, he thought to himself, *my family should know already that I've devoted my life to my son. That I don't have time for any woman — no matter how charming or beautiful — to come in and fail him like his mama did. They should know by now that it's just me and Tyson — the dynamic duo.*

Despite everything that Jason had said to the contrary, Henrietta Bullock knew the son that she had raised. *Humph*, she thought to herself. *I bet he doesn't even know yet himself that he's having feelings for this Serenity girl.*

Henrietta had been praying for her son a long time. Praying that the Lord would come in and free him from the mental bondage of his failed marriage. She'd only met the girl one time — it had been at Heavenly Blue's premiere night — but Serenity Walker had seemed like a really sweet young lady. *In fact I like her*, Henrietta thought to herself. Then she smiled. *It was something about her spirit. I like her just fine.*

* * *

"Um, it's been three days now, Serenity. You think you want to tell your best friend about the date that you went on — you know, the one that according to you, wasn't really a date?"

Serenity looked across at Jasmine as they speed-walked through the park. "Like I said, it really *wasn't* a date. But to answer your question on the how things went part—," she smiled, "—it was nice. Jason's son — his name is Tyson by the way — is a little angel. Him and Brayden got along really well."

"So are you trying to tell me that you and Jason didn't have a good time, too?"

Serenity switched her water bottle to her other hand. "Everything for us was okay. I enjoyed the show—," she grinned, "—I was pleasantly surprised that I liked it, of course. Jason said he enjoyed it, too."

"But y'all didn't enjoy each other's company though?"

Serenity shook her head. She laughed. "You're really

gonna have to quit trying to hook us up, Jasmine. Like I told you before — the man was just being nice to me. He had an extra pair of tickets. He was just being a good boss."

As Serenity upped her walking pace and began leaving her in the dust, Jasmine shook her head. "Most people I know don't go out places with their bosses," she whispered under her breath. Then she sighed. *Wish I was that lucky and he was chasing my behind instead. A man like Jason Bullock is a good catch and good men are hard to find.*

* * *

Serenity smiled at Mr. Carl and Evan as the three of them wrapped things up at the chef's station at Heavenly Blue for the night.

Carl snapped the lid onto a large storage bin and grinned. "What do you two think of the color-coded system that I put into place in here?"

Serenity nodded her head in approval. "I think it's fabulous, Mr. Carl. It's a great idea."

Evan nodded his head in agreement. "When the three of us get in here tomorrow, it's gonna make getting those plates out to all our hungry customers a whole lot easier."

Putting the finishing touches on her prep station Serenity said, "Oh, I'm not working tomorrow. I have this weekend off. Remember?"

Carl fiddled with another one of the storage bins then he glanced over at Serenity. "Oh yeah. I noticed that on the schedule. You're leaving Evan and I here to handle the weekend rush all alone." He grinned. "How did you manage to get weekends off, Serenity?" He jokingly winked his eye. "You not sleeping with the boss or something now are you?"

Carl's little attempt at humour made both Carl and Evan chuckle. Serenity, on the other hand, just smiled. She wasn't offended because she understood that her coworker didn't think anything of the sort — that he was just joking. As a natural response to his statement, she shook her head and said, "No, of course not. "

The whole time the words were coming out of her mouth, she couldn't help but wonder what Mr. Carl and Evan would think if they knew that Jason had given her Saturday off so that they could take their kids to the children's museum on that day. As for Sunday, everybody at Heavenly Blue understood that for Serenity, Sundays were off limits. She'd told Jason before he'd hired her that on Sundays, the only place she could be found was at church.

"You know I'm just messing with you don't you, Serenity?" the middle-aged Mr. Carl said with a wide smile on his dark brown face. "You're an upstanding young Christian woman — nothing like a lot of these girls I see running 'round here nowadays. Matter of fact, I'd be mighty proud if my own daughter was more like you. I know you wouldn't get yourself caught up in no mess like that. The boss either...'cause he's a decent man."

"Who's a decent man?'

Neither Carl, Evan, nor Serenity had heard Jason walk into the kitchen.

Carl beamed even harder. "You of course, boss."

Jason smiled at all three of them, then his eyes met Serenity's. "It's always good to know that somebody in the world thinks good of you."

Serenity felt like he was directing his words straight to her. She nervously lowered her eyes and focused her attention on tidying up her workstation.

Not noticing the unspoken interaction between his boss and Serenity, Carl continued on with his conversation. "I was telling Evan and Serenity here about what a stand-up type of guy you are. A person with a good soul...'bout like Serenity." He paused and scratched his head for a second or two. Then he said, "I think the two of you have a lot in common." He chuckled. "If I was in the match-making business like my wife, I'd probably hook the two of you up."

Serenity felt her cheeks begin to burn in embarrassment. Jason, on the other hand, was cool as a cucumber. He smiled at Carl. "Is that so, Mr. Carl?"

Carl nodded his balding head. "Yep."

Jason turned to Serenity. He grinned. "What do *you* think about all of that, Serenity?" He chuckled. "You think we'd be a match made in heaven?"

She honestly had no idea what to say to that one. She wiped her hands on the tea towel fastened to her waist. *Better think quick, girl*, she thought to herself. Then trying to keep the conversation as light-hearted and impersonal as possible, she laughed. "Um, I kinda like working here, Jason. From what I've noticed, employer-employee relationships never work out. When things go sour, the employee — which would be me in our case — usually ends up being fired." She chuckled again. "And like I said, I like working here."

Evan, who'd been quiet up until that moment, decided to join in on the conversation. "But what about that man who owns that software company — you know, the billionaire. He married a girl who worked for him. They've been together for over ten years. What do you think about that?"

Serenity shook her head. "That was a rare occurrence, Evan. I guarantee you it isn't the norm." She put the last utensil away in her cutlery drawer then said, "While I hate to cut this very interesting conversation that we're having short, I have to make my way on out of here. Else my babysitter's gonna be asking me for overtime. I'll see you all Monday morning."

It was true that she'd be seeing them all on Monday morning, but she also knew that she'd be seeing Jason before then. She would be seeing him the very next day when they took their kids to the children's museum. As she made a quick escape to the employee break room to retrieve her purse, she hoped against hope that Jason wouldn't say anything about their outing in front of Mr. Carl and Evan. She suspected she'd never hear the end of it from the two if he did.

As soon as she made it to her locker, she let out a quick sigh of relief. "Thank you, sweet Jesus. From the way Mr. Carl was talking, if he knew about Jason taking me and Brayden out tomorrow, I don't know when he'd ever let me live it down. That man would be trying to hook me and Jason up for all eternity."

* * *

Five Minutes Later:

Chasing Serenity

"You didn't really think I'd rat you out in there did you, Serenity?" Jason chuckled after he'd asked her the question. He'd followed her out to her car.

Serenity turned around with her hand still on her Accord's door handle. "I don't know what you're talking about, Jason Bullock."

"I'm talking about our little date tomorrow. I know you remember...we're taking our boys to the museum."

She let out a breath on a sigh. "Our outing tomorrow is *not* a date, Jason."

"Oh I know it's not a real date." He chuckled. "But I'm not quite convinced that Mr. Carl wouldn't have seen it like that. In all honesty, he's always trying to get me involved romantically with some girl or another...no matter how many times I've told him it's just me and Tyson. That I'm not interested in being in the dating game. That I enjoy being single."

A surprised look came across Serenity's face. He was probably one of the most eligible African-American bachelors in town. She never would have figured that about Jason — that he enjoyed living his life solo, just him and his son. She grimaced. *About like me and Brayden.*

"What is it, Serenity?"

She nonchalantly shrugged her shoulders. "Oh, I just

would have figured that you'd have a different woman on your arm every night."

He frowned. "Why is that?"

She squinted her eyes together as she thought of the best way to answer his question. Then she finally said, "Because...um...most women would consider you to be a good catch."

He couldn't help but smile. "And what exactly makes me a good catch, Serenity?"

"Uh...well...besides having a kid, you're everything that most single women look for."

"Is that so?" His eyes met hers. "You're single. Am I what you're looking for?"

She had no idea where he was going with his line of questioning, but it was starting to make Serenity a little unsettled for some reason. She had to inwardly tell herself to get a grip on her thoughts.

It took her a few seconds to respond. She pressed her key fob to unlock her car door. Then she climbed into her driver's seat. She closed the door, started her engine, then rolled down her window. Her eyes met Jason's, then she said, "You couldn't possibly be what I'm looking for, Jason Bullock because like you, I enjoy being single. In other words, I'm not looking for anybody. It's just me, Brayden, and God." She smiled. "Oh yeah, I also like to throw my mom and my best friend, Jasmine, in for good measure." She paused for but a moment then said, "See you at nine?"

He nodded his head. "Nine on the dot."

As she drove away, Jason couldn't help but think to himself that he was happy to hear that she was single. A surprised frown appeared on his face. *I'm living the single life. Where in the world did that thought come from, Lord?*

He shook his head. He had no answer at all.

CHAPTER 9

Serenity frowned at her son when she heard her doorbell ringing at eight forty-two the following morning. "That must be Mr. Jason and Tyson, sweetheart. They're early. Go ahead in the bathroom and wash your face and brush your teeth so we can go."

Brayden was so excited that Serenity didn't even have to ask him twice. She couldn't help but smile lovingly after her child. It normally took her two tries to get him to do those two tasks in the mornings.

As soon as she looked through the peephole and saw her mother instead of Jason standing on the other side of her door, her smile immediately morphed into a confused frown. It wasn't that she wasn't happy to see her mom — she always loved the time she spent with Betty Walker — it's just that she was surprised.

She pulled her door open so that her mom could come in.

After exchanging a warm hug with her daughter,

Betty frowned. "What's wrong, Serenity? You don't want to have breakfast with me this morning?"

It had become a Saturday morning tradition for Serenity, Brayden, and her mom to have breakfast together on Saturdays at Serenity's place.

Serenity shook her head. "Nothing's wrong mama...not really. Brayden and I just weren't expecting you to come over this morning. I thought you were going out of town with Ms. Carla. I haven't cooked anything."

Grinning and on her way to the kitchen, Betty shook her head. "I left a message on your voicemail last night that I was coming over 'cause Carla canceled at the last minute." Finally reaching her destination, Betty put on one of Serenity's aprons and smiled. She opened the refrigerator and started pulling out bacon and eggs and Serenity's special homemade pancake mix. "Don't worry baby...for the inconvenience I've caused, I'll do all the cooking this morning. Gone and get Brayden and take a seat at the table right there and relax."

Serenity was about to tell her mother that breakfast that morning wasn't going to be necessary, but then her doorbell began ringing again. "Hold up on cooking, mama. Give me a second to get the door. I'll be right back."

Serenity took several deep breaths before opening

her front door.

"Good morning, Ms. Serenity." Grinning, Tyson had beaten his father to the punchline in greeting his new friend's mother.

Serenity smiled. "Good morning to you, too, Tyson." She made brief eye contact with Jason and said, "Morning to you too, Jason."

Jason sniffed the air in appreciation. "Morning, Serenity." He grinned. "Mm, something smells good in here. Are you inviting us in for breakfast before we hit the road?"

Serenity felt like she wanted to crawl under a bus and hide. She hadn't been out with any man since she'd dated her son's father years ago. She knew that her and Jason weren't going out on a real date. She understood that she was a grown woman. But at the same time, she had no idea how her mother was going to respond to her and Jaden going on an outing with Jason. *Even if he is just a friend...just my boss.*

She didn't have to wonder much longer how her mother would react.

Betty looked at the handsome man and cute little boy standing in her daughter's doorway. She had a look of curiosity on her face. "What's going on, Serenity?"

Serenity took a deep breath to collect herself. She

smiled. "Mama, I'd like you to meet my boss, Jason Bullock and his son, Tyson." She looked over at the father and son duo then said, "Jason, Tyson...this is my mother...Ms. Betty Walker."

Hearing voices out in the living room, Brayden chose that moment to run out of the bathroom. "Mr. Jason! Tyson! I'm all dressed...let's go!"

Betty shook her head at her grandson. Then she smiled. "It's nice to meet the two of you, Jason and Tyson. I guess you're the reasons why my grandson hasn't even told his dear old grandma good morning."

With an apologetic look on his little face, Brayden rushed over and gave his grandmother a hug. "Good morning, grandma...sorry."

Betty hugged him right back. Then she turned to Jason and Tyson. "You all here for breakfast?"

Serenity shook her head. "Um, actually Mom...we're going out...um, I mean we're taking the kids to the children's museum today. We were going to catch breakfast on the road."

"No need for that. I have breakfast going already in the kitchen." She flashed them all a bright smile. "The four of you can eat right here." She turned to her daughter. "That's if it's alright with you Serenity...seeing that this *is* your apartment and all." Then she smiled over at Jason and Tyson. "And if the two want to stick around and try my food."

Jason grinned. "If what I'm smelling right now is your food, Ms. Betty, then both me and my son want to eat here. Isn't that right, Ty?"

Tyson nodded his head. "Yes, sir!"

All eyes turned to Serenity. She could tell when she was outnumbered, so smiling she shrugged her shoulders. "Eating here is fine by me."

"Good choice, Serenity," Betty said. "Now, I couldn't find a parking spot right in front of your unit, so I had to park a little ways down the lot. I have a few grocery bags of fruit that I'd like us to have with our breakfast this morning. I'd appreciate it if you took the two boys down with you and brought the fruit back in real quick."

Smiling, Jason shook his head. "Oh, I can help Serenity with that."

Betty gave him a friendly eye. "Serenity likes to buy these big ol' industrial containers of food stuffs — I guess it's because she's a chef and all. With your height and strength I could use you to open a few jars for me before breakfast and get a few things off of the top shelf. Serenity and those boys can take care of my groceries." She chuckled. "Those two are about to burst with energy and excitement anyways. They both look like they need some activity and fresh air right now."

Jason knew when not to complain with his elders. He grinned and said, "Yes, ma'am."

As soon as the front door closed behind Serenity, Brayden, and Tyson, Betty turned to Jason with a tiny smile on her face. "If Serenity had a father, he'd be the one asking you these questions, but since I'm all she's got...it's my job." Without letting her smile falter she said, "Mr. Bullock, what are your intentions with my daughter?"

Needless to say, Jason was shocked. "Intentions? Serenity...I mean Ms. Walker is my employee...I guess you could say at this point, a friend of mine."

Betty nodded her head. "Yes, I understand all of that and I mean no disrespect to you, Jason...but I wasn't born yesterday. You've only been in this house this morning for five minutes or so, and I just couldn't help but notice the way you kept looking at my daughter. There's something in your eye that suggests you want something more than just a friendship."

She let out a breath on a tired sigh then continued speaking. "Now under normal circumstances, I probably wouldn't be saying anything to you at all, but my daughter is a good woman and she's been through a lot of hurt and pain." Her tired eyes met Jason's. "You seem like a decent type, so I feel comfortable asking this of you...don't fool around with Serenity if all you have to offer her in the end is pain. That's all I'm asking of you, okay?"

Jason listened carefully to every word that Serenity's mother had said. He had major respect for a parent who would go out of their way to protect their child in such a way. He nodded his head. "I understand, Ms. Betty, and you can rest assured that I'd never hurt Serenity intentionally." Then he smiled. "I haven't known her for very long, but I've come to see that she's a very special person with a big heart. I'd never want to cause her any pain...not ever, not in any way. I can promise you that."

Betty could see the sincerity in his eyes. Pleased with his answer, she nodded her head. "I'm glad we were able to come to an understanding and you see things my way." She chuckled. "You can't tell 'cause I met the Lord and he done turned my life around. But back in my day, I didn't have too many problems with folks hurting me and mine...'cause they knew I would cut 'em. Old habits die hard, Jason. I still carry a switchblade in my purse to this day."

With that said, she turned on her heel and began making her way towards the back of the apartment.

"Now come help me with those containers in the kitchen."

As he followed her retreating back, Jason couldn't help but smile. *At least now I see where Serenity gets that little spark of feisty attitude from.* He chuckled to himself. He liked it.

* * *

Several Hours Later:

Jason grinned as he watched Serenity help their boys figure out a simple geometry problem at the children's museum. He couldn't seem to stop his mind from going back to the conversation that he'd had with her mom earlier that day. When Betty Walker had told him that she'd seen something in his eyes when he looked at Serenity, he hadn't been able to tell her she was wrong because he knew it was true.

He brought his eyebrows together in a frown. *I've only known her a short while but I think I'm starting to have feelings for her.*

"Daddy, come see what we did!"

His son's voice forced him to push his thoughts about Serenity to the side. He smiled at the three as they motioned him over to inspect their work.

Serenity's eyes met Jason's. "It's a good thing I actually paid attention in geometry class, isn't it? I never would've been able to keep up with these two in their shape-building skills otherwise."

"Did we do good, Daddy?" Tyson asked looking for approval.

Brayden of course had to follow up with, "Yeah, Mr. Jason. Did we?"

Jason high-fived both boys, then he chuckled. "I don't think I could have done a better job at building that structure myself." His eyes met Serenity's. "You two had an excellent instructor."

Serenity grinned. "It's not just any old structure, Jason. It's special." Then she looked at Brayden and Tyson. "What is it called boys?"

They both shouted at the same time, "Decahedron!"

Jason chuckled. "I'm obviously not as smart as the three of you when it comes to geometry. What exactly is a decahedron?"

Serenity was proud of both Brayden and Tyson as they shared with Jason what they had learned that day about various geometric shapes. When they were through explaining to Jason that a decahedron was a shape with ten sides, he grinned. "Now it's time for us to move on to the electronics part of the museum. I played football in college, but electronics was my major. You three need to get yourselves ready to be dazzled by my expertise."

An hour later, Serenity really was impressed with Jason's knowledge of electronics and circuitry. She grinned as he helped the boys complete some wiring and their light bulb came on. Then she clapped her hands. "Wow! Very impressive."

Jason backed away from the table and admired their collective handiwork. His eyes met Serenity's."What? You thought I was just a dumb jock?"

She shook her head. "Of course not, Jason. You're running a successful restaurant, you tutor kids at that sports clinic that you started, you're a great dad...how could I possibly think that about you?"

He grinned. "You sure?"

"Of course." She returned his smile with one of her own. "Now that we have that out of the way...you think you can show me how to make my light bulb over here work?"

In response, he came over to her little work table. "You take this blue wire here...and connect it right here."

She frowned. "Like this?"

He shook his head. Then he covered her hand with his own to show her how to make the connection.

Serenity felt an electrical shock that went straight

from where his hand was touching hers and travelled through her whole body, right down to her toes. The sensation had nothing to do with the circuitry they were working on, but everything to do with Jason's touch.

She suddenly felt her heart begin to go pitter-patter in her chest.

Jason leaned close to Serenity's ear and said, "All you do is clip the connector onto the board and it'll work. You understand, Serenity?"

"Huh? What?" She knew he was speaking perfectly coherent English, but she hadn't been able to understand a word of what he'd been saying. That's just how much an effect his touch had had on her.

He smiled. "Here, let me show you."

Perceptive of his mother's emotions, Brayden said, "Are you okay, mommy?"

I'd better get myself together before everybody starts to think I'm crazy. She quickly nodded her head. She smiled at her son. "Sure, sweetie. I'm okay."

* * *

The initial plan had been to just do breakfast and go to the museum, but the four of them ended up spending the entire day together — right into evening.

By the time Jason had dropped Serenity and Brayden off at her apartment, both boys were asleep and Serenity was bone-tired. Just like the previous weekend, Jason toted Brayden to her front door for her. When he handed the child over to her arms, he smiled. "I would come in and put him in bed for you, but I can't leave Tyson unattended in the truck."

Holding a knocked-out Brayden in her arms she smiled and said, "I understand completely."

He nodded his head. "I enjoyed our day together Serenity...I just want to make sure that you know that." He gave her a slow smile. "I'll see you Monday, okay?"

"Yep." She gave him a tiny smile of her own. "Okay."

* * *

Later on that night, after she'd said her prayers, Serenity sat up in her bed for the longest time. She was reflecting on the last month or so of her life. One thing — or rather one person in particular — kept popping up in her thoughts. And that one person was Jason.

She closed her eyes and grimaced when she thought about the moment they'd shared at the museum — the one where he'd touched her hand.

She shook her head. She'd never felt like that from anyone's touch before. *It was as if he connected with my soul on some level.* She knew at that moment that she was possibly in trouble. She knew it was very possible that she was starting to feel something for her boss. What exactly that something was, she didn't know. But one thing for sure, she was certain she didn't particularly welcome the feeling.

She frowned then said to the empty room, "Nope, I don't think I like feeling like this one little bit, Lord."

CHAPTER 10

"Can I talk to you for a minute, Serenity?"

As she loaded the dishwasher with their dishes from Sunday dinner, Serenity looked across her kitchen at her mother, who was sitting at Serenity's kitchen table.

Serenity smiled. "Since when do you ask if you can talk to me for a minute, mama?" she kidded. "You normally just go right into whatever you have to say."

Suddenly reflecting on her own words, Serenity frowned. "Wait a second, is something wrong, mom? Are you okay?"

Betty shook her head and pursed her lips into a thin line. Then she grinned. "Of course I'm okay child. What I want to talk to you about is that boy."

Serenity furrowed her eyebrows in confusion. "About Brayden?"

Betty shook her head. "Not about my grandson, honey...about Jason."

Now Serenity was really confused. "Why would you

need to talk to me about him?"

Betty sighed. Then she stood up and walked over to her daughter. She took both of her hands into hers. "I just want to let you know that I'm okay with the two of you dating. That I'm happy that you've finally managed to break free of those bonds that Brayden's no-good daddy had somehow managed to shackle on your heart."

Serenity shook her head. "I'm not dating, Jason, mom. He's just my boss."

Betty studied her daughter for a few seconds. *Lord, she's in denial*, she suddenly thought to herself. Then she frowned. "You sure about that, Serenity? I ain't gonna lie...I had my doubts when I first saw him come up into your apartment, but God done put it on my heart that you going out with Jason Bullock will be okay. Jason's one of the good guys, baby. I can tell." Then she smiled. "Plus I already warned him about that switchblade that I carry in my purse. He knows I'll cut him if he hurts my child."

Normally Serenity probably would have laughed at her mother's overprotective antics. But on this occasion, she was so embarrassed that she looked at her mother in disbelief. Then she immediately thought to herself, *Oh, Lord, my mama just threatened to cut my boss. Knowing her, she probably even said she'd cut right down to the*

102

white meat. No telling what Jason is gonna think of me now.

"You didn't really tell him that did you, mama?"

Betty nodded her head. "I sure did. It was when I sent you and the two boys out to my car to bring that fruit in for me."

Realizing that it was no use in getting herself riled up over what her mother had told Jason, Serenity simply shook her head. *After all my mama's just being herself and she said what she said out of love.*

Confirming the thought that had just gone through Serenity's head, Betty said, "I wasn't trying to embarrass you, honey. I just needed that boy to understand that I won't stand by and tolerate my baby being hurt."

Betty had to fight the tears that suddenly threatened to well up in her eyes. "I want you to be happy, Serenity. Like I told you that day you were about to move out of my house with Brayden in your belly...God can still bless you and give you a full life. I've been praying for a while now...praying that you don't end up single and alone like I've been in life. I'm thinking that this Jason Bullock might just be the answer to my prayers for you, honey."

Serenity was quick to give her mother a hug. As much as she wanted to tell her mom again that there was nothing at all between her and Jason, she held back. She knew of course that Betty loved her, but her and her mother didn't get too many tender moments like the one they were currently sharing. Serenity refused to ruin it.

* * *

Monday Evening:

"Can I talk to you for a minute, Jason?"

Jason looked up from his desk and flashed Serenity a bright smile. The fact that she had closed the door after herself when she'd walked into his office let him know that something was up.

Serenity pasted an uncertain grin on her face. "I hate to come in here so late. I know you like to leave Blue Heavenly early on Mondays. Um, I had meant to come in and talk to you earlier today, but things have just been so busy."

She could tell by this time that she was rambling, but oddly, she didn't seem able to stop herself. Jason did it for her by saying, "Is there something wrong, Serenity?"

She shook her head. "Not really. Um, I just want to apologize to you for what my mother said to you on Saturday. My mama's saved...she's really quite harmless."

He began chuckling loudly. Then he said, "You

mean she really want cut me down to my white meat?"

Realizing the ridiculousness of it all, Serenity finally allowed her facial features to relax a little. "No, she won't." Then she sighed. "Outside of Brayden's father years ago, I haven't brought any man home. I think it kind of threw my mother for a loop to see you and Tyson there in my apartment...not saying that we're dating or anything," she quickly added on.

He stretched his lips into a gentle smile. Then he got up from behind his desk and came to stand directly in front of her.

From the way he was looking at her, Serenity felt her breath catch in her throat. She was surprised as all get out when he took her hand into his.

"I've been thinking about some things, Serenity. And I want you to know that I like you...I like you a whole lot."

He sighed then continued speaking. "After my ex-wife betrayed me and left me for my teammate, I honestly thought I'd never want to let another woman anywhere close to my heart again. I figured it would always just be Tyson and me." His eyes met hers. "But after spending time with you...after getting to know you, I've come to realize that you've somehow changed how I feel about all of that."

He gave her hand a gentle squeeze. "You're something special, Serenity Walker."

By this time, she certainly didn't know what to say.

Jason continued speaking. "Now I know this has probably come as a shock to you...trust me—," he smiled, " —it came as a shock to me too when I figured it all out last night. I guess what I'm trying to say is...will you consider going out with me on some *real* dates. Will you give the two of us together as a couple a try?"

She shook her head. She pulled her hand out of his. "You're my boss, Jason. I can't...I can't do that."

He gave her a soft smile. "You remember what Evan said the other week...bosses and employees date all the time."

"That may be true, but like I said...I don't want to lose my job when we break up."

He took her hand back into his again. "But who says we're gonna break up, Serenity. I know we're early in the game, but what I feel for you is pretty strong. Plus, as a Christian man — one who really believes in the word of the Lord — I believe in being celibate until marriage. I think us not throwing sex into the mix will make it easy for you to walk away from our relationship and we still remain friends — that's if you feel like you need to."

Jason wasn't gonna tell Serenity at that moment, but

once they got together, he had no intentions of them breaking up. He never would have said anything at all to her about them dating if he didn't think they could actually make a go of their relationship and end up as man and wife. He neither believed in, nor had the time for playing games.

She shook her head. "I'm sorry, Jason. I just can't do it. Look, I have to get back to the kitchen. Mr. Carl's already left for the evening. It's not right for me to leave Evan out there doing all the cooking on his own."

After she'd rushed out of his office, he settled himself back into his chair and tented his fingers on his desk. He smiled. As a very successful ex-professional athlete, he was used to not only being competitive but also winning. He was accustomed to going after things that he really wanted.

He grinned. He refused to give up on the woman that he believed God had brought into his life for a reason.

Don't worry, Serenity, he thought to himself. *I have faith that God will work things out in our favor in the end. I think I'll back off of you a little...give you some time to think about what I said. But I'm not giving up on there being an 'us'. And I'm not giving up the chase.*

$\mathcal{C}$HAPTER 11

Since Jason hadn't said another word whatsoever about them dating and it had been two whole weeks, Serenity began to wonder if their little conversation had in fact just been a figment of her imagination.

Jasmine took a sip from her glass of sweet tea. "And he hasn't said anything at all to you since that day about y'all dating?"

Serenity shook her head. "Nope. He sure hasn't."

"That's too bad, Serenity. I really did think the two of you would make a cute couple...the perfect couple really." She began ticking items off on her fingers. "You both have five-year old boys who actually like each other. You're both saved. You've both been hurt in the past but it's way beyond time for both of you to move on." She smiled. "And y'all just plain simply look good together. Some couples are like that you know?"

Serenity herself was too busy thinking about her and Jason to fully focus on what Jasmine had just said. *I shouldn't be disappointed that he didn't try to ask me out again. I made it clear to him that I wasn't interested. But why am I here having second thoughts? Why can't I seem to get that man out of my mind?*

"Hey, girl...were you even listening to me?"

Serenity smiled. "Kinda sorta."

Jasmine giggled. "What's on your mind then? Are you over there daydreaming about him or something?"

"It was *not* a daydream. I was just thinking about him a little...that's all."

Jasmine began laughing even more. Then she wagged an accusatory finger at Serenity. "You're busted. You're not even ashamed to admit that your 'fine-as-wine' boss has you over there in a daze."

"I am *not* in a daze, Jasmine." She shrugged her shoulders. "Besides, I *do* work for him and I see him almost everyday. It's only natural for me to think about him from time to time."

"Uh, boo...I see my boss almost everyday, too. I have yet to think about the man outside of work. I think you might need to reconsider your stance on dating Jason. If I were in your position, I'd call him right now and tell him that I'd changed my mind."

Then Jasmine stuck out her hand. "Here, give me your cellphone. I'll call him for you."

"Uh, no thank you, Ms. Busy Body. Like I told you, I'm just not feeling him like that. I'm really not."

Jasmine studied Serenity's face carefully. "You sure about that, Serenity?"

"I'm a hundred and two percent positive."

"So if he started seeing somebody else...how would you feel about that?"

Serenity shrugged her shoulders. "Who Jason Bullock dates is none of my business, Jasmine. He's not mine. Why should it even matter to me?"

Jasmine lowered her eyes to her drink. She began stirring her iced tea with her straw. Then without looking up and doing an apparent three-sixty, she said, "Since you obviously don't want him, would you mind if I asked him out. I mean, could you convince him to take me to that silver and gold birthday bash that my uppity step-mama is having? She's always looking down that witch nose of hers at me since I was her husband's bastard child and my mama and me were poor. If I show up with a famous person like Jason on my arm, I can finally give her the one-up."

Serenity frowned. She wasn't exactly sure what to think of that.

"Please, Serenity. Just introduce me to him. You said that you weren't feeling him like that...I finally believe

110

you. Do your friend this one favor, girl." She grinned. "You don't even have to go through all the business of trying to convince him to take me to the party. Just get me an introduction. That's all I need." A sly smile worked it's way across her pretty face. "I can take it from there. Jason Bullock won't be able to turn all of this sexiness down."

* * *

Later on that night, after Jasmine had left her apartment, Serenity sat on her sofa Indian-style nursing a cup of sleepy-time tea. Against her better judgement, she'd agreed to introduce Jasmine to Jason. *Lord, introducing Jasmine to Jason shouldn't even bother me. How come I feel some type of way about agreeing to introduce them though?*

She shook her head. She frowned.

* * *

The Next Day:

"Hey, Serenity. Come on in. What can I do for you this afternoon?"

Serenity stepped into Jason's office. She gave him a

tiny smile. "Well, Jason...I was kinda wondering if you could do me a favor."

He nodded his head. "For you, of course." Then he chuckled. "Just as long as it's not illegal, I'd be happy to help you out. What is it?"

"I promise you that it's not illegal and well, it's not really for me. It's for a very good friend of mine. She's been a fan of yours for years and she was wondering if I could somehow snag her an introduction."

Jason chuckled. "I didn't exactly know I had fans anymore. I've been out of the pro football league for several years. I thought everybody had just about forgotten about me."

Serenity couldn't help but shake her head in disagreement. "Um, you're one of the most winningest quarterbacks of our decade. I honestly don't think anyone is going to forget about you for a very, very long time. Especially those three back-to-back touchdowns that you ran all by yourself in the Super Bowl during your last year in the league."

"You know, Serenity...I never would have pegged you as the football-loving type. You seem a little too ultra-feminine for that. Now keep in mind, I see nothing wrong with a woman being ultra-feminine. In fact, I kinda like it."

She blushed.

He smiled. "Did I call it? Is it confession time?"

"Okay, okay Jason. To be absolutely honest with you, I didn't follow football until we met — well, until shortly after we met. About a month ago, Mr. Carl and Evan pulled up some video clips on the internet from some of your games. Bottom line — after watching you play — I was hooked."

He grinned again. "In that case then, I'll do that favor for you and meet your friend. But in return you have to agree to go to the Cardinals preseason game with me this weekend." He reached into his desk drawer. "I have two tickets right here. They're good seats. You'll get to see all the action...up close and personal." Jason couldn't help thinking that for him, being up close and personal with Serenity would be the best part of their little trip to Charlotte.

In all honesty, Serenity had been itching to go check out her very first pro football game. Her eyes met his. She smiled. "Good seats you say?"

He nodded his head. "Yep. The best."

"Okay, Jason. What's a football game between friends? You've got yourself a deal."

* * *

Chasing Serenity

Two Days Later:

Jasmine pulled her sexiest dress out of her closet. After she'd stepped into the slinky fire-engine red sheath, she couldn't help but smile in approval at her reflection in her full-length mirror.

"Yep. This will just about do the trick," she said to the empty room. "This little number right here hits my curves in all the right places." She rubbed her well-manicured fingertips down the side of her hips. "Yep, no man will be able to resist me in this."

Minutes later, as she stepped out of her apartment, she couldn't help but think how excited she was to be finally meeting Jason Bullock.

She grinned to herself. *After all, the man's practically a freaking superstar. Serenity's a fool to be turning that sweet, irresistible hunk of chocolate down.*

* * *

The second she introduced Jasmine to Jason at a secluded little table in a corner of Heavenly Blue, Serenity had to fight to stop the scowl from forming on her face.

Jasmine looked up into Jason's eyes with a sweet

little smile on her cherry-red painted lips. "Wow, it's a real pleasure to meet you, Jason," she practically purred. "You're even more handsome in person than you are on the TV screen."

Then she reached out and squeezed one of his biceps. She let out a sexy little giggle and nodded her freshly-weaved and curled head in approval. "And I see you're still keeping your football-season body intact, too."

When Jasmine put her hand, with its fresh-from-the-salon manicure, on Jason's arm, Serenity narrowed her eyes in disapproval. *Dang, Jasmine is just going all out with the flirting. She has absolutely no shame.*

Quickly trying to make her face look as neutral as possible, Serenity gave both Jasmine and Jason a tight little smile and said, "I hope the two of you enjoy your dinner this evening. I'm gonna have to excuse myself. I believe I'm wanted in the kitchen."

After she'd slung the thirtieth plate down on the waitstaff table with a little bit too much force, Mr. Carl turned to Serenity with a look of concern on his face. "Everything alright, babydoll?"

Not able to kick her funky mood, Serenity gave Mr. Carl a smile that she hoped didn't look too fake and said, "Everything's just fine. Peachy really."

Mr. Carl took her comment at face value, even

though he knew something was the matter. Minutes later, he turned to her and said, "This bad mood you're in...it don't have anything to do with the boss out there wining and dining that dimepiece do it?"

Serenity stopped in the middle of the plate of herbed salmon that she was preparing.

From her tell-tale action, Mr. Carl nodded his head. "Yep, I thought so." He continued piling food onto the plate he was getting ready. "I was out in the dining area a few minutes ago, and I can tell you that the boss ain't feeling that girl like that. She's beautiful and all, but it's like he's got his mind on something — or rather *someone* else he'd like to be sitting across from instead."

When Serenity didn't say anything, he continued on speaking. "Now I'm not trying to get all up in you and the boss' business, but I know that man has feelings for you, girl. It's probably about time for you to get over whatever is holding you back and stop turning a good man down...before it's too late."

* * *

Later on that night, as she lie in her bed, unable to get to sleep, Serenity couldn't stop the bad feelings she was starting to have for Jasmine.

"Lord," she said out loud, "Jasmine knew how I felt about him. Despite everything I was saying, Jasmine knew that I was falling for Jason. I know she did." She shook her head. "I just don't understand how someone who says they're my best friend and that they love me could try to push up on someone I was feeling like that."

She laid there with her eyes closed talking to God for several minutes. When she finally lifted her eyelids, she had one thought on her heart. *There's only one logical solution. I'm gonna have to tell Jasmine how I feel about Jason and we're gonna have to go from there. I can't simply deny this feeling that I'm having for him anymore. I don't care if the whole world knows I'm falling for him. After all, confession is good for the soul.*

As she finally fell asleep, Serenity had a smile on her face. She was sure that no matter what happened, God would have her back.

CHAPTER 12

"Right now? You have to come over to my place and speak to me right now? It's six o'clock in the morning, Serenity."

Serenity nodded her head. Then she moved her cellphone to her other ear. "I know that, Jasmine. But what I need to tell you...well, it's best if it's not said over the phone. And it's best if we have this conversation right away."

Jasmine yawned. "Okay, girl. Come on over. Bring me a cup of coffee from Mickey D's...the one down the street from your place. See you in twenty."

* * *

Fifteen Minutes Later:

The first thing Jasmine said when Serenity stepped into her living room and handed over her cup of coffee was, "He said no. Can you believe it?"

Serenity frowned. She didn't feel like being sidetracked off of the subject she'd come there to talk to Jasmine about. She wanted to cut straight to the chase. Deciding to oblige her anyways she said, "Who said no, Jasmine?"

"Jason. That's who. He said he couldn't take me to my uppity stepmother's birthday party."

Deep down inside, Serenity wanted to do the happy dance from Jasmine's little response, but out loud she said, "Jason is actually what...I mean *who* I came over here this morning to talk to you about."

Jasmine frowned. She allowed a confused expression to wash over her face. "Why would you possibly want to talk to me about your boss?"

Serenity's eyes met Jasmine's. "Because Jasmine...I have feelings for him. I'm standing in your face, woman-to-woman, telling you to back off." Her voice didn't waver when she paused then continued speaking. "Now I know you and I have never been in a situation like this before — you know, where a man is between us — but since I met him first, I think I have priority...that I have first dibs."

Not once in their ten-year long friendship had Serenity ever talked to Jasmine like that. Jasmine smiled to herself. *I guess because I never tried to step on her*

119

turf like I did last night with Jason.

Serenity was confused when Jasmine didn't say anything. She frowned. "Well, Jasmine...what do you have to say to all that?"

Jasmine took a tiny sip of her coffee. "I say okay I guess. He's all yours, Serenity. Evidently he wasn't interested in me anyway. Is there anything else you need to tell me?"

Serenity shook her head. "Nope. That's it."

Jasmine nodded her head. "Alright. I guess I'll see you some time later."

* * *

As soon as Serenity walked out of her front door, Jasmine ran and picked up her cellphone. She dialed Jason's number. As soon as he answered his cell, she added another caller via three-way. Then she said, "Jason...Ms. Betty...our little plan worked!"

Serenity's mom beat Jason to speaking. "You mean to tell me she's changing her attitude about Jason?"

Giggling, Jasmine nodded her head. "She sure did. She basically told me she's gonna kick my behind if I don't back off the man she's interested in." Jasmine couldn't stop giggling. "I thought she was gonna run to my bedroom and set that little red dress I had on last night on fire."

At that moment, Jason chuckled into the phone. He liked the sound of all of that. He knew that he now had a real chance to prove to Serenity that he'd fallen in love with her.

"Ms. Betty—," he said in a serious tone over the connection, "—I'm gonna try my best to make sure you don't have to cut me. That alright with you?"

Betty couldn't help but chuckle in response to his question. She'd had a long talk with Jason and she knew exactly how he felt about her daughter. She was sure she didn't have to worry about him breaking Serenity's heart.

Smiling, she said into the phone, "I'm gonna hold you to that Jason Bullock. I'm gonna hold you to that."

All he could say was, "Yes, ma'am."

* * *

For Serenity, Saturday couldn't come soon enough. Now that she had admitted to herself how she was really feeling about Jason, she could barely wait to let him know. Of course she was nervous about the entire situation, but she knew she had to get everything out in the open. A tiny part of her was afraid that he'd changed

121

his mind about wanting them to date. However, she knew she couldn't let her fears stop her from telling him the truth. *The worst that can happen is that he'll say that he's not interested*, she reasoned to herself.

She sighed as she put the finishing touches on her makeup. She couldn't remember the last time she'd taken so much care in her appearance and she was glad that her hard work showed. She nodded her head in approval. She knew that her look was on point.

Then she frowned. *The only bad thing about my situation is that I can't call and talk to Jasmine about it.* She shook her head. *Lord, please let Jasmine and I find a way to work past all of this. Good friends should never let a man come in between them.*

The sound of her doorbell ringing put a halt to her thinking about her problem with Jasmine. She took a deep breath and pulled open her front door.

Jason couldn't help but smile in approval. "Wow, Serenity. You sure know how to make a pair of jeans and a football jersey look good. By the way, I love your Cardinal spirit and I brought you this gift. I think you're gonna like it."

Serenity looked at him in surprise as he handed her a thin, flat jewelry box.

"Go ahead...open it. It won't bite you. I promise."

Chasing Serenity

In all honesty, Serenity loved presents so she couldn't keep the smile from popping up on her face. She slowly lifted the lid. Then she chuckled. "It's a very beautiful necklace, Jason. I guess it's a good thing I'm a Cardinals fan."

Jason reached out his hand and picked up the 14 karat gold chain from the box. It had the Cardinals team logo etched onto a heart-shaped charm dangling from it. "I'm glad you like it. It actually matches your earrings. Here, let me help you put it on."

Serenity lifted her ponytail to give him easy access to her neck.

The minute his fingers brushed against her skin, Serenity felt that same sensation she'd experienced when he'd touched her hand while helping her with the circuits at the children's museum.

She closed her eyes and willed her heart to stop beating so fast.

Jason fastened the clasp on the necklace, securing it around the column of her delicate throat. Then he pulled back and frowned. "Are you okay, Serenity?"

She quickly nodded her head. Then she smiled. "Yes, I'm just fine. Let me get my purse and we can hit the road."

As soon as they pulled out of her driveway, Serenity

looked over at Jason and grinned. "Good thing we don't have the boys with us today. They'd be a little ticked that you drove this convertible instead of the truck."

He grinned. "I bet they would. We'll have to let them tag along with us to the next Cardinals game — when the regular season starts next month." Then he chuckled. "I love my son more than any Earthly thing, but it just wouldn't be a real date with kids underfoot."

His comment — specifically the real date part — made Serenity feel encouraged. She clasped her hands together in her lap and looked down at them. "So are we on a real date, Jason?"

He took his right hand off of the steering wheel and covered both of hers. "Of course we are, Serenity. I know it's been awhile since I asked you about dating me, but I hope you didn't think I was actually going to give up on us. I was just trying to give you some time to figure out what I already had figured out...that we have something special between us." He didn't add on the other part he was thinking — the part about how he knew they belonged together — because he didn't want to scare her away again.

She absolutely had to make sure that they were on the same page. "Does that mean that we're exclusive, or does it mean that you're seeing me and other people?

Other women."

He gave her hands a gentle squeeze. "For me, that means we're exclusive, Serenity. I don't intend on having eyes for any other woman but you."

"What about Jasmine?"

He smiled. "Your friend is a nice girl, Serenity. Maybe I'll even introduce her to my younger brother. But I'm not interested in dating her...only you."

"You sure?"

He nodded his head. Then he chuckled. "I have to be sure. Else your mom is gonna cut me."

Serenity smiled. Then she laughed. "Alright. I believe you. I guess it's official then...we're on a date."

* * *

Serenity really couldn't remember the last time she'd had so much fun with someone of the opposite sex. *So much fun with anybody period*, she thought to herself as she laughed at one of Jason's ridiculous jokes.

He brought his Mercedes Benz convertible to a smooth stop in her driveway. He compressed a button and let the roof down, exposing them to the pleasingly warm night air.

She sighed. "I'm going to have to get me one of

these one day...I mean the convertible part...not the Benz part."

He smiled. "What? You don't like Mercedes?"

She shrugged her shoulders. "I can't rightfully say yes or no. Before today, I'd never rode in one. And I've never driven one." She smiled. "Although I've always wondered what it was like driving a Benz."

When he immediately hopped out of the car and came and opened the passenger-side door, she looked at him in confusion. She wasn't expecting their date to end quite yet. *Oh evidently, he must have somewhere to be,* she thought to herself.

"Okay, my sweet Serenity. Wonder no more—," he began escorting her to the driver's side of the vehicle. "Get behind the wheel and take me for a spin."

* * *

A Half Hour Later:

Jason chuckled as Serenity finally brought the car to a stop in her driveway. "Dang, girl," he said, "we're gonna have to get you to a race track."

Serenity didn't normally have a lead foot, but her little Honda Accord only had four cylinders. Jason's Benz had eight. In other words, the convertible was plenty powerful and she surprisingly loved that feeling of raw energy at her fingertips. *Or rather under my feet*, she thought to herself with a smile.

She shook her head. "Now you have to believe me on this...I normally don't drive like that, Jason. Safety is usually first with me."

He patted her hand reassuringly. "It's okay, Serenity." He chuckled. "You were only doing ten over the speed limit. I've seen plenty of people doing double that. And I could tell that you're a good driver."

She smiled. "Since my trusty ol' Honda is on it's last leg, I'm looking into getting a new car some time soon. I'm definitely gonna make sure I get something with a little more power than my Accord. Nothing as fancy as this, of course. But six cylinders for sure."

He frowned. "Your car still giving you problems? That's why it's not here in your drive?"

She sighed. "Unfortunately, yes." Then she giggled. "You wouldn't happen to want to give me this as a loaner would you? I promise I'll take real good care of her. I'll return her without so much as a teeny-tiny scratch."

He was quick with his reply. "The key's already in your hand. I have my truck and another car in my garage. Sure...she's all yours."

Serenity hadn't been expecting him to say that. She'd

only been joking. She quickly waved her hands in protest. "Oh, no, Jason. I was just kidding around. I can't let you do that."

He smiled. "Why not? Like I said, I have other vehicles I can drive." Then he winked his eye in the semidarkness. "Plus, Tyson would probably be your best friend forever. You having this car means he gets more chances to be taken out in the truck." With that said, he chuckled. "I think you remember exactly how much he loves that."

She shook her head. "I can't, Jason."

"Yes, you can." He paused for a moment then said, "Let me do this one thing for you, Serenity. It makes me feel good to be able to make your life a little better...a little more comfortable." He shrugged his shoulders. "I know you'd do the same for me if the tables were reversed." He chuckled again. "At least I hope you would."

He could tell that her resolve was slowly loosening, crumbling like dust. She gave him a playful little slap on the arm. "Of course I would, Jason Bullock and I guess I'll take you up on your offer — but only for a few days until my car gets fixed mind you."

"Does that mean you'll drive me home tonight...or do I have to walk?" he teased.

She giggled. "I think you've been a good boy lately — especially since you showed me such a good time today on our first official date." She revved the convertible's powerful engine. "Yeah, I believe I'll drive you to your place."

* * *

Twenty Minutes Later:

Serenity looked around her surroundings in awe. "Wow, Jason. When you said you lived out in the 'burbs, I didn't think you meant like *this*. It's nice out here. I like it."

Jason grinned in appreciation. None of the women he'd dated in the past — including his ex-wife — would have ever gotten excited about his large country-style modern home that was nestled in a cozy little secluded thicket of tall evergreens. They would have said it wasn't polished or sophisticated enough.

Serenity pointed towards a gap in the trees closest to them. "Is the lake part of your land, too?"

He nodded his head. "Yep."

"I can imagine that Tyson loves it out here."

He chuckled. "And you would be right. I can barely keep him indoors in the summertime. He seems to think there's too much to do outside."

"I don't blame him one bit, Jason. If I were a kid, I'd be out here in all of this all day, too." She laughed. "Probably even all night. Trying to catch fireflies in the dark...maybe even taking a dip in the lake."

He grinned. "In that case...want to be a kid again?"

She glanced over at him with a questioning smile in her eyes. "Be a kid again?"

"Yep. Come on, Serenity...let's run to the lake...let's have some fun. I know you can't tell from this angle because of the trees, but I had a nice wide path put in. It'll lead you right to the water's edge. It's a very short distance. Beat you there? The winner gets to choose our next date destination."

He was surprised when she jumped out of the car and began flying down the path. "The little cheat," he chuckled under his breath as he sprinted out of the convertible and gave chase.

Barely panting, he caught up with her just as she made it to the water's edge. He wrapped his arms around her waist from behind and bent his head down close to her ear. "You know I let you win...right?"

Serenity's heart was racing in her chest from her exertion, but the sensation of his warm breath on her earlobe made her heart beat even faster.

He said it again. "You know I let you win...right?"

Her voice was low and husky, barely audible when she said, "No."

It was then that he noticed the sensual tension that was between them. If he was honest with himself, he would have admitted that it had always been there, right from the beginning, just waiting for the right moment to surface.

He knew he'd fallen in love with Serenity. He knew that standing there holding her body close to his had put him in a danger zone of sorts. *Lord, give me strength to keep my hands to myself*, he said inwardly as he slowly let his arms drop from around her waist.

Serenity felt as if someone had removed her favorite warm, comforting blanket when she felt him end their embrace.

Jason took a deep breath to try to clear his head while at the same time understanding that what he really needed was a cold shower. He frowned. He felt like a prepubescent teenager, one who'd just discovered the mystery of male-female attraction. *She probably should just push me into that lake. That'll do the trick. That'll get my hormones to go down.*

It was a warm evening, but missing the feel of his touch, Serenity wrapped her arms around herself. Staring out over the perfectly calm water of the lake that was shimmering like glass in the moonlight she said, "This looks like a good place to come and think. You ever just come out here and think, Jason? You ever do that?"

He smiled. He nodded his head towards a bench that had been placed on a pier to their right. "Actually, Serenity, I like to come out here when I'm troubled...you know, to talk to the Lord and pray. That's why I put that bench right there."

She began walking towards the bench. He followed her. He smiled and motioned with his hand for her to sit down. "Ladies first."

Serenity settled herself on the seat and he sat down beside her. She smiled. "You must have some phenomenal parents. They raised a son with good manners."

He grinned and took her hand into his. "My mother and father would be proud to hear you say that. It took them a whole lot of trying and determination, but I think they managed to instill the fear of the Lord into all of their kids."

"It's six of you...right? You have five sisters and brothers that is?"

He nodded his head. "Yep." Then a faraway expression came into his eyes. "I always imagined that I would someday have a large family of my own — just like my parents had. After my ex left me, it took me awhile to wrap my mind around the fact that it was just gonna be me and Tyson."

Serenity understood completely. "I understand, Jason. Like I told you, I'm a single child. I always figured that someday I'd get married and have a brood of kids of my own — two boys and two girls, of course." She sighed. "Like you, I had to finally face the fact that it was just gonna be Brayden and I."

He gave her hand a gentle squeeze. "You were never married?"

She shook her head. "Nope. I thought I was going to be though — to Brayden's father — but he failed to tell me that he was already in a committed relationship. His 'I-love-yous' and his 'we're-gonna-be-a-family' were all lies." She sighed. She shrugged her shoulders, glad it only hurt a little bit to talk about it at that point in her life.. "I guess you could say that he just wanted to use me for the sex. My mother tried to warn me, but I wouldn't listen...I thought I was in love."

He had to know, so he asked her the question that was pressing on his mind. "Do you still love him, Serenity — Brayden's father that is?"

She shook her head. She smiled. "Nope. I haven't

seen him since the day I told him about Brayden. He said he wanted nothing to do with our child. That was six years ago."

Jason knew the pain that came from knowing that your child's parent had rejected him or her. He'd been through it all with his own son. As much as he wanted to tell Serenity that he loved her and wanted them to be together — that he wanted them to create that big family that they'd both dreamed of — he knew things were too early in the game. He had to settle for offering her his empathy instead.

His gave her hand a gentle squeeze, one that he hoped communicated just how sorry he was for both her and Brayden. "You know that bonehead of an ex of yours is the one missing out don't you? You're a great catch and Brayden is a great kid. I'd be proud if he were my son." *And if you were my wife.*

She smiled. "You're pretty awesome yourself, Jason Bulluck...that little gentlemen that you've raised so well is awesome, too. I'd be proud if Tyson were my kid." Then she giggled. "I don't think we should tell either of ours boys any of that just yet. I'm pretty sure they'll both try to get us married off. I heard Brayden whisper to Tyson at the children's museum that he wished he was his brother."

Jason chuckled. Then he stood and reached for her hand to help her up from the bench. "I think you're probably right and both of us should probably get home before our kids somehow find a way to send a posse looking for us."

She laughed right along with him. She couldn't agree more.

CHAPTER 13

"Well, Serenity, it's been two weeks since you told me that you and Jason been dating...how are things going?"

Serenity looked across her mother's kitchen table at her and smiled. "Trust me, mama...you're not gonna have to cut him."

Betty laughed at her daughter's little statement. Then she said, "So things are going good between the two of you?"

Serenity let out a breath on a contented sigh. "Yeah, I believe they are." She couldn't hold her feelings inside any longer. She had to talk to somebody since her and Jasmine hadn't been talking like they'd used to. She frowned. *Jasmine and I don't really communicate with each other, ever since I told her to back off of Jason.* Then she smiled. "Mama, I think I'm in love with Jason." She shook her head. "No — correction — I *know* I'm in love."

Betty was all grins from her daughter's comment. "That's wonderful news, Serenity!" She came over and gave her daughter a warm hug. Then she pulled back wearing a puzzled expression on her face. "You said you love him. How come I sense there's something wrong?"

I should've known my mama was gonna notice. I never could get anything past her...not even as a baby. Serenity grimaced. "It's not Jason that's the problem — even though he does indirectly have something to do with what's troubling me. The problem is me and Jasmine."

"You and Jasmine?"

Serenity nodded her head. "Yeah...me and Jasmine." Then she sighed, mentally preparing herself for what she wanted to say. She took a slow sip from her coffee mug. "Last month...before Jason and I became a couple...Jasmine asked me to introduce her to him. Long story short, I did just that. However, the night that I introduced them, I realized that I had feelings for Jason myself and I told Jasmine to back off — that I had met him first."

Betty knew all about what her daughter had just told her. In fact, it had been partly her idea to get Jasmine to push up on Jason in the first place. She'd hoped that it would shock Serenity into realizing how she truly felt about the man. And now Betty was glad that the little plan that she, Jasmine, and Jason had come up with had worked.

As much as she wanted to get everything out into the open, Betty understood that Jason and Serenity's relationship was too new for her to comfortably say anything about all of their matchmaking efforts just yet. She didn't want to give her daughter any type of reason to turn away the man she loved. Betty smiled to herself. *I'm not giving her any excuse to push away the man who loves her right back.*

Betty lowered her eyes and looked into her cup of tea. "Are you mad at Jasmine for talking to him, baby? Do you feel like she did you wrong...stepped on your toes?"

Serenity sighed. "I ain't even gonna try to lie, mama...at first I was. I was mad at her. But that feeling only lasted for a hot second."

"Since you ain't mad at her, why don't you just let Jasmine know? Tell her just like you just told me. Get everything out in the open." She covered her daughter's hand with her own. She smiled. "Trust me...you and Jasmine have been friends for a long time. You two are gonna work this thing out." Then she chuckled. "You're gonna get to keep your man, Serenity, and your best friend too."

Chasing Serenity

Later on that evening, as she drove over to Jasmine's apartment in Jason's loaner Benz, Serenity prayed that her mother had been right.

* * *

Jasmine couldn't stop the grin that appeared on her face when she looked through her peephole to find Serenity standing on her front stoop. She was genuinely glad to see her bestie on the other side of her door. Due to their supposedly strained relationship over Jason, they hadn't seen each other in two weeks. To Jasmine, two weeks without talking to her best girlfriend was a long time.

Despite how much she wanted to give Serenity a hug, she forced herself back into the role of scorned best friend that she was supposed to be playing. She pasted an emotionless expression on her face, pulled open her door and said, "Hey Serenity. Long time no see. What can I do for you today?"

Serenity sighed, thinking to herself that this was going to be harder than she thought. "Um, I was wondering if we could talk."

Jasmine waved her hand in the entrance. "Come on in."

They sat side by side on Jasmine's sofa. Serenity sighed. "I think we need to clear the air between us. And I need to get some things off of my chest 'cause I'm not interested in losing you as a friend."

"Uh...okay."

Serenity nodded her head then continued speaking. "I want you to know that I was offended when you tried to hit on Jason. That I felt like you knew that I liked him but you pushed up on him anyways. I think you were wrong for that."

For once, Jasmine was glad that she'd taken that one acting class in college. She pulled out the big guns and forced tears to glisten in her eyes. Dabbing at her eyes with the back of her hand she said, "Say no more Serenity. I owe you an apology for all of that. I hope you can find it in your heart to forgive me and we can move on as friends."

Seeing Jasmine cry made Serenity do the same. Seconds later found them hugging each other in a sisterly embrace, both with tears in their eyes.

Grinning and thankful to God that her and Jasmine were back on the good foot, Serenity pulled back and smiled. "I missed talking to your behind something fierce, Jasmine Monroe. You better not ever pull a stunt like that again."

Jasmine gave Serenity another heartfelt hug. "I missed you too, boo and trust me I won't." She grinned. "I really *am* happy that you found Jason. I can tell you're in love with him...it shows all over your face. Let me run to the kitchen and get us some snacks. I know I missed out on a lot the past few weeks. We've got a whole lot of catching up to do."

As Jasmine disappeared into her kitchen, Serenity couldn't help but smile. "Lord, I'm glad that my mama ended up being right this time. Good friends are hard to find and I definitely didn't want to lose my girl Jasmine." She sighed then said, "She's more than a friend, she's like a sister to me."

CHAPTER 14

"You know you didn't have to do this...right?"

Jason smiled over at Serenity. "I know I didn't *have* to do it, but I wanted to. Today is our official one-month-of-dating anniversary. I wanted to celebrate."

They were sitting out on the covered patio of his spacious home, watching the sunset over the lake. They had what appeared to be a scrumptious meal on the table in front of them.

Serenity poked at her coq au vin using her fork. Coincidentally, the wine-braised chicken dish was one of her favorites.

"You work so hard at Heavenly Blue feeding everyone else sweetheart, that I figured it was about time that someone turned the tables and did the same for you. You know...gave you some tender loving care." He grinned. "You're not scared to try my cooking are you, Serenity?"

She laughed. "Not scared, Jason. Just cautious." She shrugged her shoulders. "I understand that you own a now very reputable restaurant and all, but I haven't once seen you cook anything."

He couldn't help but chuckle. "Okay, okay. You got me on that one. I'm a food lover for sure, but definitely not a chef. I do alright cooking for me and Tyson, so this meal that we're sitting in front of should be edible." He winked his eye at her. "Plus, I'm gonna confess — since I wanted our anniversary date to be perfect, I had plenty of assistance from Mr. Carl with the cooking."

Serenity smiled and began slicing into her meat. "In that case, Jason, since we've already blessed the food, let's eat."

He chuckled while she continued carving into her meat. Then she said, "You and Mr. Carl...you guys seem really close."

Jason smiled. "We are. He's like a second father to me. Him and my dad were friends in the Army years ago. They were both stationed at Fort Bragg together and got shipped overseas together."

"Oh, I didn't know you were a military brat, Jason."

He shook his head. "I'm not. My dad only did two tours of duty. When my mother popped out her second kid — which was me by the way — he decided that he

143

didn't want to be dragging us around the country. He really enjoyed the military, but he sacrificed his happiness for my mama and us kids."

That's the type of man I'd want in me and Brayden's life, she thought to herself. *One who'd sacrifice his well-being and aspirations for the ones he loved.* She suspected that Jason was the same way as his dad. *I'm sure Jason would give his all — his everything — to make his wife and kids happy.*

A little under a half hour later, Serenity was full and satisfied. A semblance of a smile danced across her lips when she heard her favorite mellow jazz piece piping through the patio's stereo sound system. "Mm-mm-mm...dinner was delicious, Jason. My compliments to the chef. Thank you."

"Oh, you're welcome, sweetheart."

"You're setting the mood with some of my favorite songs this evening." She grinned. "If I didn't know any better, I'd think that you had downloaded my favorites playlist from my streaming music account."

He chuckled. Then he smiled. "Nope. It's just a case of great minds thinking alike."

She was surprised when he stood up from the table and reached out his hand. "This one is my favorite. May I have this dance?"

Chasing Serenity

Jason held Serenity close to his heart as they swayed in unison to the slow, soulful melody. To him, that exact moment in time was perfect. He wished he could bottle how he was feeling that very minute and keep it forever. True, he'd been married before and had dated extensively in his lifetime. But he'd never felt for his ex-wife — or any other woman — what he was feeling for Serenity. *Lord, she completes me.*

Serenity sighed and laid her head against Jason's chest. She'd only known him a little over three months, but she'd never felt safer, more at peace than she was feeling at that very moment.

He leaned in closer to her ear. "I want to thank you for giving me — for giving *us* a chance, Serenity. For letting me get to know you and Brayden better. For letting me into your life."

She felt the exact same way. *I somehow feel like I should be thanking him instead,* she thought to herself. Out loud she said, "You don't have to thank me, Jason. I get mutual pleasure from being around you and Tyson."

A slow smile made its way onto his lips. He was pleased with her answer. They stayed there dancing until the last strains of the melody faded away into the night air. Jason reluctantly broke their embrace and placed his palm gently on the curve of her cheek. "I feel so lucky,

Serenity, so blessed to be with you like this right now. You're saved, generous, kind-hearted, loving, gorgeous...the total package. Everything in a woman I could ever want or need."

As he was caressing the side of her cheek with his hand and slowly dipping his face towards hers, Serenity felt her breath catch in her throat. *He's gonna kiss me, Lord.* She hadn't been kissed by a man in years. She didn't have but a second or two to contemplate what was going to happen because it only took Jason a second or so to softly cover her lips with his own.

Every nerve ending in her body reverberated as he placed his palm on the small of her back and deepened their kiss.

To Jason, kissing Serenity was like being hooked on an intoxicating drug. He felt addicted to her. He wanted more and more. He just couldn't get enough. "Oh, Serenity, my sweet serenity," he murmured against the soft skin of her neck when he finally pulled his lips away from hers.

Her breath was coming in ragged little bursts. She'd been kissed before in the past, but no kiss had ever made her feel quite like this.

Tyson was spending the night at his grandparents house so Jason's home was empty. He loved Serenity. He wanted her in the most intimate way. The only thing that was keeping him from doing what his sinful flesh wanted to do was his oath to God and his promise to her to keep things celibate between them.

He had to use all the determination within himself to break their embrace. He gave her a tiny smile. "My lovely Serenity...I think I'd better get you home."

From the way things were getting all hot and heavy between them, she couldn't agree more. *Lord, seeing that I'm not interested in breaking my vow of celibacy, him taking me home right now is probably for the best.*

* * *

Over the next month or so, Jason and Serenity spent as much time as possible together. In fact, they saw each other almost everyday. However, for safety's sake, Jason had decided to try his best to limit their time alone.

He was only a man and he knew he was in love with Serenity. Bottom line, it was getting more and more difficult for him to keep his hands to himself.

Fortunately for him, Brayden and Tyson accompanied them on many of their outings. In fact, Jason was spending so much time with Brayden that the little boy was starting to feel like he was his son.

Chasing Serenity

Jason smiled across his office in Heavenly Blue at Serenity then said, "Trust me, sweetheart...Brayden will have fun."

Serenity glanced over at Jason with a dubious look on her face. "Are you sure about this? That it'll be safe?"

Jason's brother, Paul, owned a luxury speedboat and jet skis. He'd docked his boat on Jason's lake for the weekend because the men in Jason's family were having a men's only day out on the water.

Jason walked over and pulled Serenity into his strong arms. He dropped a soft kiss on her lips then pulled back smiling. "I love Brayden, sweetheart...just like I love you. I wouldn't let anything happen to him out on the lake. He'll have a lifejacket on the entire time. He'll be safe."

Serenity was so focused on the safety aspect of their conversation that she totally missed the part where he said he loved her. She frowned. "You sure about that?"

He nodded his head. "I know I've never told you this before, but I was on the white-water rafting team in college as well. In other words, I'm very familiar with the water. Sweetheart, both our boys will be safe."

He finally convinced her with his last couple of statements. Then, with her mind relieved of her worry for her son's safety, what he'd said only a minute earlier finally clicked in her brain. "Wait a minute...did you say you loved me?"

He grinned and pulled her back into his arms. He tilted her chin up so that he could look down into her gorgeous dark brown eyes. "Yeah, sweetheart. I love you, Serenity Walker. Like I said, I love Brayden, too."

That had been the first time that Jason had ever told her that he loved her. She would have confessed the truth, which was that she loved him and Tyson in return — that is if he hadn't reached into his pants pocket and pulled out a black velvet ring box.

The diamond ring sparkled in the light of the room as soon as he opened the box's lid. Serenity's heart began beating at what felt like a thousand beats per minute. *Oh my God...sweet mother of Jesus. I think he's going to ask me to marry him.*

"Serenity Diane Walker...will you be my wife?" He waited several seconds for her to respond. When she didn't say anything at all, he smiled and said, "Well, what do you say, sweetheart? Serenity, will you marry me?"

She was so much in awe that she hadn't heard a word of what he'd said. All she'd heard was mumbles. "What?"

He smiled again. "Will you marry me, Serenity? Will you make me complete? Become Tyson's mother while I become Brayden's dad. And then later on, we can get a couple of add-ons and create that big family that we'd both dreamed about. I love you, baby. Please say yes."

Tears of pure joy were beginning to wet Serenity's cheeks when she nodded her head and shouted, "Yes! Yes! Yes! Yes! Yes!"

At that point, Mr. Carl stuck his head through Jason's office door. He hadn't even knocked first. He began chuckling. "If the two of you were in the world, I'd have to have assumed that all that shouting and commotion was the two of you in here getting your freak on. But since y'all both trying to serve the Lord, I'm gonna guess that you busted out that ring that you bought the other day, and that she said yes."

Serenity waved her left hand up in the air while beaming from ear to ear. "He sure did, Mr. Carl. And yep, I said yes!"

Grinning, Mr. Carl came in and patted Jason on the back. He gave Serenity a warm hug then he chuckled. "I guess me and Evan and the rest of the staff are gonna be catering a wedding!"

* * *

The Next Day:

"Oh my God, Serenity...that rock is gorgeous!" Serenity smiled as her mother and Jasmine admired the engagement ring that Jason had given her.

Jasmine gave Betty a sly look then smiled. "Now that the two of them are engaged, you think it's safe to tell her?"

Serenity pasted an inquisitive grin on her face. "Tell me what?"

Chuckling, Betty nodded her head. "Since you're the one she was mad at, Jasmine, I'll let you do the honors."

If she wasn't curious before, now she was dying to know exactly what her mother and her best friend were talking about. "Okay, you two. What gives?"

Jasmine began giggling. "You're gonna like this, Serenity. You really are, boo."

Serenity shook her head. "Well, I don't see how I'm gonna like it if nobody's gonna tell me about it. Now tell me already."

"Okay, okay," Jasmine said. "Here we go."

Exactly three minutes later, Serenity shifted her eyes between her mama and Jasmine while wearing a look of disbelief on her face. "You mean to tell me you guys set me and Jason up? You were just coming on to him, Jasmine, to make me jealous? You were trying to make me see what I was about to miss out on? You weren't interested in him at all?"

Both Betty and Jasmine nodded their heads. Then Betty said, "It was my idea, baby." She chuckled. "But Jason was in on it, too. Looks like to me we were on the right track, 'cause everything worked out just fine in the end. You two are getting yourselves hitched."

Grinning, Serenity couldn't help but shake her head and say, "I should be mad at all of y'all — Jason included." Then she laughed. She pointed an accusatory finger at Jamine. "You especially, Jasmine Monroe. Now I've already forgiven your behind for stepping up to Jason like you did 'cause I love you, girl. But I'd be lying if I said it's not good knowing that my best friend didn't really disrespect me like that."

Jasmine giggled. "I'm sorry I had to put you through all of those emotions, boo. You want a hug?"

Serenity smiled. "I deserve a group hug from both of you."

As her two favorite women in the world encircled their arms around her, Serenity felt thankful that God had chosen to put the both of them in her life.

She sighed in contentment. *Very grateful indeed.*

CHAPTER 15

From the minute she and Jason had announced their engagement, both of their families had gone into wedding planning mode. Specifically Jason's mother, Ivory, and Serenity's own mom.

Serenity grinned at Jason as they sat together on the bench at his lake. Given all the action going on from planning their wedding, the two of them had finally found a rare occasion on which to spend some quality time alone.

He took her hand into his and gazed up into the starry night sky. "I'll always consider right here to be our spot, sweetheart."

"Our spot?"

He nodded his head. He smiled. "Yep."

"Why is that Jason?"

He let out a slow breath on a sigh. "Because...the first night I brought you out here to this lake was the night I realized I wanted to make you my wife."

She leaned her head over onto his shoulder and stared at the night sky with him. "That was months ago, sweetheart, and you'd just met me. You knew you wanted us to get married way back then?"

He nodded his head. "Yep. I knew back then." Then he grinned in contentment, thinking back to that evening that seemed so long ago. "That night, Serenity — that moment — will always be in my heart."

They sat there in companionable silence for several minutes more, just enjoying each other's company and their beautiful surroundings.

Then she sighed, thinking about him, her and their families. "I remember you mentioning that you have five siblings. I've met all of them except your younger sister. That must have been a remarkable feat on your parent's part — you know, raising five upstanding citizens and all."

He nodded his head. Then his eyes took on a faraway expression as he looked out over the tranquil lake.

"What's wrong, Jason?"

He shook his head. "Nothing really, babe."

"You sure? It seems like there's something weighing on your heart." She gave his hand a gentle squeeze of encouragement. "I've been told in the past that I'm a good listener if you want to talk about it."

Thoughts of his sister, Lexi, who was the closest to him in age, began to come to his mind. He sighed. "I was just thinking about my younger sister...that's all."

Serenity allowed a tiny smile to work across her lips. "You mean the one who likes horror movies?"

"You remembered."

She nodded her head, thinking about the day months earlier when he'd asked her to call him by his first name. That had been the day that he'd told her that his sister was a fan of horror flicks. "Of course I remembered, Jason." Then she smiled.

There was something about his wife to be, something that pulled on his soul and just made him feel comfortable sharing his innermost demons with her. He sighed. "My sister and I used to be really close, but we're not anymore. He pursed his lips deep in thought then continued speaking. "I try to not judge people — I know that's the Lord's job — but I just can't help but rebuke Lexi's lifestyle."

"Her lifestyle?"

He nodded his head. "Yeah. Now don't get me wrong...she's a sweet girl...but for me, that all goes out the window when a man or woman is fooling around with somebody else's spouse. My parents taught all of their kids better than that."

Serenity understood that cheating was wrong. She was against it herself. Based on Jason's strong emotions, she couldn't help but wonder if his ex-wife had done the same thing to him — if that was part of the reason that his disgust for a sister that he apparently loved so much was so strong.

He shook his head. "I could never be with a woman who slept with another woman's man. I just couldn't do it."

Serenity frowned, thinking about her own situation from the past. Thinking about Brayden's father who'd been very married when their son was conceived. "But what if the woman or man didn't know that the other person was married?"

He let out a little bark of laughter that was full of displeasure. "Oh, I think deep down inside, a person always knows. They may not want to admit it to themselves, but I'm sure they know. Like I said Serenity...I could never be with a woman who'd slept with another woman's husband. There's a fundamental dysfunction to a person who's like that. A malfunction in their soul...one that I just don't want to deal with."

It was at that moment that Serenity realized that she and Jason would never be able to make a go of their relationship. *I'm that other woman that he's talking*

156

about, she thought sadly to herself. *There's no way I could keep a secret like that in my marriage. He's never gonna accept me for who I am — he just said he wouldn't. I'm going to have to let him go.*

She'd been so happy the past few weeks — ever since she and Jason had gotten engaged. Now she felt like someone had reached up into the heavens and stolen the sun right out of her bright, happy sky.

Noticing that something had changed in her mood, Jason frowned. "Is everything okay, sweetheart?"

Serenity pulled her engagement ring off of her finger. She pressed it into his hand. "I'm sorry, Jason. But I can't marry you."

He was so shocked and confused that he simply stared after her as she sprinted towards her car. By the time he'd recovered, her taillights were disappearing into the night.

* * *

Two Hours Later:

Jasmine shook her head. "I just got off the phone with Jason, Serenity. He said you wouldn't answer your door for him or accept his calls. I just don't understand, sweetie. Why did you give Jason his ring back?"

Chasing Serenity

Serenity dabbed at the tears in the corners of her eyes as she and Jasmine sat on her bed together. She shook her head. "It's over, Jasmine. He doesn't want a woman like me."

"That's ridiculous, Serenity. That man loves you. He just got finished telling me so himself."

By this point, Serenity felt like she didn't even have anymore tears in her eyes to cry. "He said he could never marry a woman who'd slept with a married man...a woman like me."

Jasmine shook her head. "You didn't know Jonathan had a wife, Serenity. I'm sure Jason would understand that."

Serenity had to fight a new wave of tears. Her voice choked when she said, "Jason said he wouldn't. He said deep down inside I knew about Jonathan's wife. That I just...I just...I just didn't care!" At that point, she really started bawling like a baby. Loud, sorrowful, heaving bouts of tears that ripped from the depths of her very soul.

Jasmine placed her arms around her bestie and let her cry her heart out. She was downright mad at Jason for hurting her friend. She narrowed her eyes in anger. *I don't mind if Mama Betty cuts his uppity, ex-football playing, 'holier-than-freaking-thou' behind. I might even get me a switchblade myself!*

$\mathcal{C}$HAPTER 16

The pain that Serenity felt from breaking up with Jason was the worst thing she'd ever experienced in her life. It hurt ten times worse than Jonathan deceiving her. The only thing that kept her going and halfway sane was Brayden.

Speaking of Brayden, Serenity knew that her son was deeply affected by her and Jason's breakup. Brayden had been looking forward to having not only a father, but also having Tyson as a brother. Serenity was sure that Tyson felt the same. That he'd been looking forward to her becoming his mom and the four of them being a family. She felt herself tearing up again. *He even told me so*, she sadly thought to herself.

She shook her head while sitting alone at her kitchen table thinking about it all. It had been two days since she'd given Jason her ring back and she was scheduled to work at Heavenly Blue that very day.

She stood and slowly walked out of her kitchen. She

frowned as she bent down and picked up her official resignation letter from her living room table. She'd initially wanted to just mail it to Jason. However, at the last minute, she'd decided that she refused to be a coward and that she would deliver it in person.

She grimaced thinking back to months earlier when she'd told Jason that she hadn't wanted them to begin dating. She'd told him up front that if things went sour between them, she'd lose her job. He'd insisted that wouldn't be the way things worked out. That they'd walk away as friends in the worst case scenario of a breakup.

She shook her head. She didn't see them ever having any type of relationship again. *Not even a casual friendship. My heart won't be able to take it.*

She frowned and tucked the resignation letter into her bag. "I guess I was right after all."

* * *

Jason knew that Serenity was at his office door, even before he heard her knock. That's just how in tune to her he was. He didn't know why she'd decided to come see him, but every part of him was glad that she had.

He closed his eyes, simply savoring the sensation of being in the presence of the woman that he loved with all his heart. She looked so beautiful and vulnerable standing there that all Jason wanted to do was to go to her and wrap her in his arms. "Sweetheart," he said. "I'm glad to see you. Come in...we need to talk."

From the second she stepped into his office, Serenity knew it had been a bad idea to deliver her resignation in person. All the way along the drive over, she'd given herself a series of pep talks — all in an attempt to convince herself that she was ready for seeing him. She'd honestly thought that she was prepared for their face-to-face meeting. Now that she was looking at him in the flesh, she knew that she'd been lying to herself the whole time.

She took a deep breath, stepped into his space and closed the door behind her. "I've come to turn in my official resignation, Jason. I thought it only right that I did it in person."

Frowning, Jason took the piece of paper that she was handing him from her fingers. He didn't even look at it. He dropped it on his desk. "I don't want your resignation, sweetheart. I want us to talk. I need to know why you gave me your ring back...why you want to leave me. Whatever the reason, I'm sure we can work it out."

She shook her head. "I don't think so. I think it's best if we just leave things the way they are."

He came over and took her hand into his. "You do still love me don't you, Serenity?"

She closed her eyes. She felt her heart breaking a thousand times just from feeling his touch. "You have my resignation. I have to go, Jason."

She tried to get away from him, but he wasn't loosening his grip on her hand.

"Please don't leave me, Serenity. Please, sweetheart." His voice broke with emotion when he said, "I love you too much."

By this time, Serenity had tears in her eyes. "Love is not enough, Jason."

"Baby, love is everything. God so loved the world, that he gave his only begotten son. That proves that love is everything, sweetheart." He reached over and began gently wiping the tears away from her eyes using the pad of his thumb. "Let's just talk. We can work this out."

She shook her head and used all the strength in her body to finally break her hand away from his grip. "No we can't work it out, Jason! You don't want me! That woman that you said you could never marry...you know the one who slept with a married man...the one who is dysfunctional with zero morals...she's me! She! Is! Me!"

As the woman he'd lay his life down for ran out of his office, he finally understood why she'd broken up

162

with him. He was stunned. He was in disbelief that his sweet serenity would be a cheater. He didn't like the situation, not one little bit.

Feeling empty, he walked over to his office's window and look mindlessly out onto the cityscape. "But, Lord I still love her."

* * *

A Week Later:

Paul smiled over at his brother as he missed sinking the ball into the basket. "Man, Jason, I know football is your thing, not basketball...but that was an easy shot. You just gave me the game."

Jason shook his head and began walking towards the sidelines. He hadn't really been interested in a game of one-on-one anyways.

As they were walking off of the empty court towards the bleachers, Paul gave Jason a brotherly pat on the back. "I know this all has something to do with you and Serenity breaking up. Want to talk about it, bro?"

Jason frowned. "There's really nothing to talk about, Paul. We're not together anymore. End of story."

Paul shook his head. "I just don't understand, man. Serenity's nothing like your ex-wife. None of us in the family really thought you should've hooked up with Andrea's gold-digging butt. Now, Serenity," he smiled, "Serenity on the other hand...she's a real sweetheart. I'd be proud to call *her* my sister-in-law."

Jason zipped up his gym bag with a little too much force. Then he said an almost-curse word under his breath when he noticed he'd torn the zipper-pull partially off its track.

Paul chuckled while Jason scowled. Jason shook his head. "When it comes to Serenity, everything sweet and innocent isn't always what it seems. 'Bout like Lexi."

Paul let a breath out on a sigh. "Bruh, I already told you that you need to lay off of Lexi for being with Mike. Dude didn't tell her he was married. And by the time she found out, she was already in love. Plus, you know him and his wife were already getting a divorce because his wife was sleeping with everything on this side of the Appalachians."

Paul frowned. "Now, back on topic, are you trying to tell me that Serenity was fooling around with a married man?"

It was Jason's turn to grimace. "Apparently so."

"Did you get the details? You know, find out the circumstances behind why she did it?"

An emotionless expression made its way across

Jason's face. "I didn't need to know details, Paul. The fact that she was with some other woman's husband is all I needed to know."

Paul let out a breath on a worried sigh. "I'm gonna tell you something, Jason and I hope you listen. Serenity is a good woman. She's faithful, beautiful, kind, loving and the list goes on and on. There are many a man out here who would stand in line to be loved by a woman like her — and I'm not talking just physically. I mean loved mentally, emotionally and spiritually. She's not your ex, man. She's not Andrea. I'm a hundred and thirty percent sure there's a good explanation as to why Serenity did what she did. You say you're saved, yet you don't have a forgiving heart. What happened to letting God be the judge of folks' wrongdoings."

Paul slung his gym bag over his shoulder and began walking away. Then he turned back around. "Real talk, bro...you're about to lose a good thing because you're stuck on stupid." He shook his head. "Dang on shame, man."

Jason stood there with a scowl on his face watching his brother's retreating back. Then he tilted his head and knitted his eyebrows together. A little voice inside of him finally said, *what if Paul's right.*

* * *

Later on that evening, Jason took an early shower and got down on his knees to pray. At first he hadn't wanted to give what his brother had told him any credence. He hadn't wanted to admit Paul may have been right. But eventually some sense had kicked in and he'd decide to take everything that Paul had told him to heart.

He lowered his his chin to his chest in complete surrender...in total submission. "Now I need you Lord to intervene in my affairs and show me the way."

When he got up off his knees minutes later, he had tears in his eyes. God had put it on his heart that he'd been wrong. *I was wrong in my approach to my sister, I was wrong in how I was treating Serenity. I was wrong in it all.*

A half hour later as he laid in his bed wide awake with thoughts of his beautiful Serenity on his mind, he frowned when he heard his doorbell ringing. A quick glance at the clock at his bedside showed that it was still early in the night. It was only a little after nine o'clock.

He pulled a pair of sweats on and a tshirt. He padded to his front door. When he looked out of the peephole and saw Betty Walker standing there on his stoop clutching her purse that was slung over her shoulder, he frowned.

"I see your shadow in the sidelights of your front door, Jason. Open up. You and me need to have a little talk."

Jason narrowed his eyes in concern. He was a fit guy — still had his athletic form — but he imagined he'd get hurt up somewhat if Betty Walker pulled a switchblade out of that purse that she was holding on to for dear life.

Betty began wagging her finger at Jason's front door. "Now open up, boy. Like I said, I see you in there."

Jason shook his head and cracked his door open. Seeing his line of vision fall cautiously to her handbag, Betty cut her eyes at the man who had broken her daughter's heart into a thousand little pieces. *Not to mention that grandson of mine.*

Deciding to offer an olive branch, she gave him a tight little smile. Yeah she was smiling, but she still had a look of displeasure in her eyes. "If you're worried about me cutting you, you can take my purse or I can take it back to my car. But you and me need to discuss some things."

Jason opened his door wider. As soon as Betty walked in he said, "Ms. Betty, before you say anything, me and Serenity breaking up was all my fault and I know now I was wrong. And I intend on fixing it." He gave her a cautious smile. "I'm doing it tomorrow — fixing things between the two of us that is. If you want to have a seat, I'll tell you all about my plan."

As she made her way through his spacious foyer to his living room, Betty had to hide the smile that was trying to work its way across her lips. *Lord, thank you for intervening in this situation. I knew you'd come through for my child 'cause you're always right on time.*

CHAPTER 17

The next morning, Serenity was glad it was a Saturday. It meant she didn't have to get out of bed early to get Brayden ready for school. Missing Jason was hurting her something bad and she was going to relish the time alone.

She'd bawled her eyes out so much in the past week that she no longer had tears left to cry. All she had was an empty feeling. One that she suspected would never completely go away. She frowned. *Not even in time.*

Seconds later, when her cellphone rang the first four times, she decided to ignore it. When the number of calls coming to her device had reached about twenty in less than five minutes, she picked up the phone. She couldn't help but hope that it was Jason calling her wanting to work things out.

Seeing that she'd missed calls from Jasmine, her mother, Jasmine's mama, Carl, Evan, her pastor, her first lady, and a slew of other people she'd met in her day-today life — all within four minutes — she knew something was up.

"What in the world is going on, Lord?" she said out loud as she pressed the dialer on her cell to call Jasmine back first.

"Serenity! Turn you TV on to BET...do it right now!"

Serenity felt a sinking sensation in her soul. She didn't know what was happening, but she couldn't imagine that it was good.

"Girl," Jasmine said excitedly, "you're not going to believe this!"

Jasmine was talking so fast and with so much enthusiasm that Serenity couldn't get a word in edgewise. She simply picked up her remote and turned the TV on.

What she saw when her television screen lit up made her jaw drop and her heart lurch in her chest. Evidently BET was doing a live special coverage news event and they were right outside her house — literally right outside her door really.

"Girl! You see it?! You see what I'm talking about?!"

The cameraman zoomed in on Jason and celebrity news reporter, Gina Amberville. Gina smiled into the camera. "For all you viewers who just joined us, we're here with our favorite ex-Cardinals quarterback, Jason Bullock. We're standing outside the front door of his ex-fiancee, Serenity."

Gina then turned to Jason and put the mic in his face. "I understand that you dropped the ball on your engagement to Serenity and now you're trying to make a quick save...is that right, Jason?"

Jason nodded his head and smiled into the camera. He pulled out a black velvet ring box. Serenity suspected that it contained her engagement ring. Then he said, "I messed up big time, Gina. As many of you already know, my first marriage ended badly. I've been scarred ever since. When I met Serenity a few months ago, she showed me that I was worthy of a good woman's love." He shook his head and frowned. "Problem was, deep down inside I was scared of our relationship failing and ending badly like my first marriage did. I mentally pushed Serenity away. But through lots of prayer I've come to realize that Serenity is my heart." He stared directly into the camera lens. "I know you're watching baby, 'casue I just got a text on my cellphone from your best friend, Jasmine. She said you're right there in the house with your TV on. Please forgive me, sweetheart. I'm doing this on national TV because I want the whole wide world to know just how much I love you...how I feel about you. Please open that door, sweetheart. Come out here and tell me that you forgive me. That you'll take this ring back and become my wife."

The cameraman zoomed back in on Gina and she began speaking. "We're gonna be here live on location for at least the next ten minutes. Our toll-free number is scrolling at the bottom of the screen as well as our online address. Call us! Hit us up on social media! Let us know if you think Serenity is gonna take our friend Jason here back!"

"Serenity, Serenity!" Jasmine yelled excitedly into her phone. "What are you gonna do, girl?!"

By this time, Serenity had tears in her eyes. "I love him, Jasmine," she whispered. "I want him back."

Jasmine laughed into the phone. "Hurry up then. I know your butt just rolled out of bed. Run into the bathroom, brush your teeth, throw your hair into a ponytail — use that fancy silver scrunchie thing, you're gonna be on national TV you know, put on those designer jeans that I gave you last Christmas and the matching blouse. Then run your behind on out the house!"

Five minutes later, every single one of the TV station's millions of viewers got the answer they were waiting for. When Serenity opened her door and flew straight into Jason's arms with tears running down her cheeks, everyone knew her answer was yes.

*E*PILOGUE

Lexi Bullock gave her brother Jason a thumbs up as he and his blushing new bride made their way onto the dance floor for their first dance as husband and wife. Lexi had been very surprised and grateful when her big brother had called her two months earlier and apologized for pushing her away like he had. He'd admitted that he'd been wrong. He'd told her that whatever sin she was committing was between her and God. Of course Lexi had informed him that she'd already repented of her sin and that she and her lover had put a stop to their relationship until he was officially divorced. She smiled thinking about her man. They'd made plans to marry the day after his divorce was finalized.

Jason grinned down at his lovely wife. He leaned into her ear and began whispering. "You look very beautiful today, Mrs. Bullock. Thank you again for forgiving my biased thinking and marrying me anyways." In classic Jason style he then chuckled and said, "Although I know I would have chased you forever until you finally leaned over to my way of thinking."

She couldn't help but grin, she knew he would have. She believed him.

As she caught a glimpse of their two boys high-fiving each other for some reason and scarfing down copious amounts of wedding cake, she couldn't help but sigh in contentment and sheer happiness. She knew that God had blessed her with the family she'd always wanted. And she was sure that more blessing were on the way.

Always aware of her emotions, Jason held his wife even closer and whispered into her ear, "What's wrong, sweetheart? Having second thoughts already?"

She sighed again, then smiled. "Nope. No second thoughts here, babe There's absolutely nothing wrong...everything's perfectly alright. I was just thinking how glad I am that my mama didn't cut you where she wanted to cut you. That's all."

Ironically, it was at that moment that Jason happened to glance over at Betty. She was looking at him out of the corner of her eye. He chuckled again. "Me, too, sweetheart. Me too."

FIRSTMAN PUBLICATIONS

Thank you very much for reading this book. On the following pages, we have provided previews of other great books by this author — stories that we feel you will thoroughly enjoy. Also, feel free to visit our website at **W W W . F I R S T M A N B O O K S . C O M** to:

*Register for FREE offers

*Sign up for our mailing list

*Check out additional great books by other Firstman Publications featured authors

*Order a FREE catalog

OTHER BOOK BY TARETHA JONES
Because Chivalry is not Dead
Saving Charmaine
Even if the Winds Still Blow
Loving Jasmine
Finding Faith
Romancing Monica
Faith Through the Fire

Taretha Jones Books In The *Heaton Family & Friends* Series

EVEN IF THE WINDS STILL BLOW   *PAPERBACK ONLY $9.95*

Item Code: TAJO001

The lovely Irene Madison thought that she would never find her soul-mate. A string of failed relationships and promises not kept, made her doubt that Prince Charming even existed...existed for her that is. In walks Edward Heaton into her life. He's battled his demons and is convinced that Irene is his true love...the one that God had prepared specifically for him. But will he be able to convince Irene that they have a love that will endure the winds of change, even to the end of time?

BECAUSE CHIVALRY IS NOT DEAD *PAPERBACK ONLY $9.95*

Item Code: TAJO002

Tabitha Jenkins' life is left in shambles after her marriage to her abusive husband, Dr. Xavier Carrington, fails. Homeless, jobless and almost penniless, will she be able to trust in God to turn her situation around—and will she have the faith to let go of the demons of her past, and learn to love again.

From the day he'd met her a year ago, Dave Heaton had known there was something special about the beautiful Tabitha Jenkins. After suffering a failed first marriage to an unfaithful ex-wife, will Dave allow his distrust and hurt to destroy everything God is waiting to bless him with.

SAVING CHARMAINE   *PAPERBACK ONLY $9.95*

Item Code: TAJO003

Charmaine Heaton is a young, beautiful, God-fearing photo journalist with a feisty attitude, but a heart of gold. When she involves her best friend's brother Devin — a victim of a troubled childhood — in her plans to travel on assignment to war-torn Afghanistan, she discovers that he's the love of her life. But, will she be able to convince him that he is worthy to be loved and that their love is worth fighting for.

Firstman Publications   www.firstmanbooks.com

Chasing Serenity

DATE: _____

Firstman Publications, P.O. Box 14302, Greensboro NC 27415
www.firstmanbooks.com
Email: firstmanpublications@gmail.com

BILL TO
NAME _____ COMPANY _____
ADDRESS _____
CITY _____ ST _____ ZIP _____
Phone( ) _____ Fax( ) _____ E-Mail _____

SHIP TO
NAME _____ COMPANY _____
ADDRESS _____
CITY _____ ST _____ ZIP _____
Phone( ) _____ Fax( ) _____ E-Mail _____

Book Title	Item Code	How Many	Price Each	Total Price

☐ Money Order enclosed payable to Firstman Publications -OR-

Credit Card Number _____
Name on Card _____
Expiration Date _____ CVV Code _____
Signature _____

TOTAL AMOUNT	
SHIPPING: $3 for one book. $1 each additional book.	
SALES TAX: N.C. Add 7%	
GRAND TOTAL	

Chasing Serenity

Chasing Serenity

A FINAL MESSAGE FROM THE AUTHOR

Thank you for reading this book. I am wishing each and every one of you PEACE, LOVE, & BLESSINGS!

Chasing Serenity

Made in the USA
Las Vegas, NV
05 July 2023

74266333R00111